Kathryn Lomer was born in north-west Tasmania and lives in Hobart. Her novel for young adults, *The Spare Room*, became a Children's Book Council Notable Book for Older Readers 2005 and was also shortlisted for the Adelaide Festival Awards for Literature, the *Courier-Mail* Book of the Year Awards and the Children's Peace Literature Awards 2005. Her most recent collection of poems, *Two Kinds of Silence*, was published in 2007. Her first collection of poetry, *Extraction of Arrows*, won the Anne Elder Award and was shortlisted in the John Bray Award for Poetry and the *Age* Book of the Year Awards. Her poems have also been awarded the Josephine Ulrick Poetry Prize in 2000 and the Gwen Harwood Poetry Prize in 2003.

T0307406

Also by Kathryn Lomer

Fiction

The God in the Ink

Young Adult

The Spare Room

Poetry

Two Kinds of Silence

Extraction of Arrows

[CAMERA OBSCURA]

KATHRYN LOMER

UQP

First published 2008 by University of Queensland Press
PO Box 6042, St Lucia, Queensland 4067 Australia

www.uqp.uq.edu.au

© Kathryn Lomer 2008

This book is copyright. Except for private study, research, criticism or reviews, as permitted under the Copyright Act, no part of this book may be reproduced, stored in a retrieval system, or transmitted in any form or by any means without prior written permission. Enquiries should be made to the publisher.

Typeset in 12/17 pt Granjon by Post Pre-press Group, Brisbane
Printed in Australia by McPherson's Printing Group

Australia Council for the Arts

This project has been assisted by the Commonwealth Government through the Australia Council, its arts funding and advisory body.

Cataloguing-in-Publication Data
National Library of Australia

Lomer, Kathryn, 1958- .
Camera obscura.

ISBN 978 0 7022 3597 9

I. Title.

A823.4

For Louise and Adrienne

Contents

Camera obscura

How does light look when left entirely to itself?

If you look into an empty box full of light and the light is not reflected on surfaces, you will see blackness. Only when there is an object for the light to fall upon can we see the presence of light.

Do you have any rooms? *Ci sono camere libere*?

The woman looks up from where she is wiping down tables on the terrace of the pensione. She is in shadow. A thick, green vine covers latticed timber, letting only speckles of light through here and there. Bunches of grapes hang thickly, bursting.

I step out of the brilliant sunlight into shade. The cool of the shadowed air is a relief on my skin.

She looks me up and down surreptitiously, winding a loose strand of blond hair into position behind her head. Perhaps her hair is in a bun or a French twist of some kind. I know after seeing just this one gesture, that it is habitual. It is a graceful movement.

Yes, we have some rooms. But perhaps not as cheap as you are after.

She has taken in my backpack, my travel-weary jeans, my unruly hair.

I do not want the cheapest room on the island, I say. What I'm after is a beautiful room with a desk. And a reasonable price.

The woman laughs at this and says that I will not know if it is a reasonable price unless I see the room and decide whether it is beautiful or not.

She gestures for me to take off my pack and follow her.

The Pensione Ulysses is cool. The floors are terrazzo, liver pink with inlaid flecks of colour. I want to lie down on the smooth surface, as if in a river, and let the coolness flow over me, washing away the dust, the heat, the tiredness. The sadness.

She says over her shoulder, I think I have just the room for you. She pushes open a door and I see a desk below a window with dark green shutters angled out towards each other, creating lines and triangles of light. The bed has an iron frame and a cobalt blue cover. There is a big armchair.

The woman says a price – much cheaper than rooms nearer the beach – and raises her eyebrows. I nod.

My name's Carita, she says.
Karen.

I unpack my camera bag carefully and lay out all the lenses on the desk. I put my clothes in the cupboard and my backpack under the bed. I feel at home. I take out my diary, my hairbrush, my photo of Ralph, his photo of the aurora australis.

September 16th
I have found a beautiful room with a desk. It is a five minute walk to the beach and a forty minute bus ride to Nuoro, the village where Grazia Deledda was born. I am so tired from the trip and from speaking Italian that I will have to sleep.

When I close my eyes in the big iron bed the pattern of light from the shutters remains on my retina. I think about getting up to close them completely but the thought drops into the darkness of sleep.

The courtyard terrace is transformed when I come downstairs. Fairy lights are strung among the vines and a candle burns steadily on each table. There are six tables but only three are occupied. Two are piled with plates of food and wine bottles, and flanked by young Italians looking assured, brown and beautiful. Their voices rise in friendly altercation and laughter. At the third table Carita is sitting with a man wearing impeccable summer clothes. His face looks as if some sculptor has scraped away too much clay trying to give definition to the cheekbones. There are sharp shadows on either side of his face. Carita looks up and sees me hesitating in the dark oblong of the doorway. She beckons.

Karen, I would like you to meet Don. Why don't you join us? That's much better than sitting alone, isn't it?

By all means, do join us, says Don in a smooth English voice. His eyes are gentle and I can see fairy lights reflected in the pupils.

For fifteen hundred years after Plato, it was thought that a gentle fire glowed out of our eyes, illuminating what we saw, creating vision.

Carita has gone into the kitchen where somebody – a man – is singing an altogether different song from the one coming from speakers in the courtyard. The recorded song is a syrupy Italian melody. The one in the kitchen sounds like Greek – something discordant and Middle Eastern about it.

I look at Don and we smile about this cacophony as he pours wine into my glass.

That's Antonio, he says. Carita's husband. He's the chef.

Is he Greek? Antonio sounds Italian.

To his eternal sorrow, no, he is not Greek. But he pretends. He sings Greek songs, quotes Greek poetry and philosophy, cooks Greek food when he gets the chance and always, always, uses Greek olive oil in the kitchen. He says it is imbued with all the wisdom and energy of the Greek culture, that the olives are grown on land watered by the tears of wise men. He is rhapsodic about Greece.

They say the quality of the light in Greece is like nowhere else.

They do, indeed, say that.

How much light is there?

Carita brings plates of food to the table. Grilled octopus, Greek salad. She shrugs her shoulders. I must indulge him, she says. This is what he wants to cook, he says, to put himself in a good mood after all that pasta. So, please eat with us, Karen. Tomorrow will be time enough to choose your own.

Antonio joins us, taking off his apron with a sweeping gesture and tossing it on the concrete of the terrace. He looks about sixty, full of energy; his skin is the colour of the brine from black olives. He serves out the octopus. Carita gets up to collect dishes from one of the other tables and to bring coffee for the guests.

Antonio says, So, you are the photographer?

I must have looked startled.

Carita went up to your room to ask if you wanted dinner and she assumed you must be sleeping. She pushed your door open a little bit to check and saw your camera gear on the desk. Is that your job or just a hobby?

It is my passion.

It's my job. Mostly.

And what will you photograph here in Sardinia, may I ask? The bare rocks, the dust?

I'm here to take photographs for a book about Grazia Deledda. A new biography.

Ah. Grazia Deledda. Yes, Sardinia's famous daughter, says Antonio. Our Nobel prize winner. There is a festival, you know. In her honour. But you have missed it. A pity.

I didn't want photographs of the festival. I want photographs of the places that inspired her. *And the light.*

Antonio and Don nod.

Antonio says, What about a photograph of my wife? She is beautiful, no? She still inspires me after all these years.

We all look to where Carita is laughing at one of the tables. It is true. She is beautiful.

She is not Italian, I say.

Oh my goodness, no, says Antonio. She is my northern goddess. A Finnish Swede to be exact. She comes from a place where in summer light lasts for twenty-four hours. But we met in Greece. Only good things come from that country. When I met her she was as green and fresh as the purest virgin olive oil. She lit a fire in my heart. It is still burning. He turns to Don suddenly. Ah, my friend, I am sorry, he says putting his hand on Don's shoulder. Let's have more wine.

September 17th
I discovered tonight that Don flew here in his own plane. He does this twice every year, once in April and once in September. He is retired, widowed. Such words these are; they only describe what he isn't. Much harder to say what he is. Sad, perhaps. Certainly, sad.

My intention has been to stop on the coast for a few days to rest and relax, spend time on the beach after a long southern winter, swim. Instead I find I stay at the pensione, reading or talking. Carita, Antonio, Don – together they have an unusual energy. There is something rare here.

Whoever is free sits with me. They seem happy to open up about themselves. Of course I miss my homeland, Carita says. Little things – the light over the lakes in summer. Ice on the rivers. But I was an outsider anyway, a Finlander. My mother and father spoke Finnish, which is not related to other Scandinavian languages. We are all outsiders in one way or another, displaced, not belonging in the way we might want. So, in some sense it is easier to be an outsider here, openly, obviously.

Don tells me that his flying began in the RAF during the war. He was a bomb aimer, flying Lancasters over Germany, riding in cramped space at the bottom of the fuselage. Frostbite was common. Those bombs caused people to lose limbs long before they were ever dropped on the earth. A WRAF officer was sent to plan heating systems for the bombing hole and Don fell in love with her. Her name was Norah. She didn't notice him at the time but, among other things, Norah organised a dance. Don played the piano on the night and won her heart. Later she told him she couldn't help but notice him under the spotlight. He says there was no spotlight that night. Norah took him home to meet her mother even though her mother had said, Don't expect me to like him. What can be so special? Soon her mother was feeding him rationed bacon and mysteriously acquired eggs.

I became more afraid then, Don says, when I had Norah. Of course I didn't tell her that. And she never showed her anxiety. She told me, though, when the war was over, that every time we took off on a raid into Germany, she went to the end of the runway in the dark, stood there and prayed. We were married for thirty years. I miss her. I miss her.

How does love look when left entirely to itself?

September 19th
Don has asked me to go up in his plane, fly over the island. I don't know if I can tell him that I'm afraid. He says we should go at dawn and see the sun come up, that it looks like it's coming to meet you.

During the war we flew without lights, and those on land were blacked out. We relied on our navigational instruments. But sometimes panic would settle on me there in the dark, in the noise and vibration, and I'd think, We are lost, we will always be lost.

September 20th
I still have not been to Nuoro. I didn't realise how much I needed this kind of space and rest. Since Ralph left I have worked and worked and I haven't let the hurt in. Or let it out.

Don must have guessed that I'm afraid. He does not insist, but the offer is still open.

Ra was the Egyptian sun-god. The sun was an eye. When it opened it was day; when it closed it was night.

He wrote to tell us, you know, two years ago when it happened. We were having lunch when the letter arrived. Antonio read it to me. It said, *My world has come to an end. How can I go on living? She was the light of my life.* We just looked at each other across the table. What can you say?

September 21st
We choose to share our lives, want to, madly, feel bereft if we do not. But how we set ourselves up. How we invite desolation. An end will come and not together unless you have the will to make it so. Oh, Ralph. You weren't mine in that way, not my husband, not my anything. You were my love.

I have been at the pensione for a week when, in the waters off Finland, a ferry hits an iceberg and capsizes. The ferry was taking a group of Finnish Swedes back to their homeland for a visit. The aurora borealis, the newspaper says, was magnificent that night and people would have been on deck watching it. They would have seen the iceberg. There were no survivors.

Carita wears black for three days. She tells me the Finnish name for the aurora. Fox fire. According to a Finnish legend, Repu is a fox and this is his tail swishing a fire, not of heat but of light.

In Tasmania I have seen the aurora three times. The first time was terrifying, not knowing what the veils of red and green light could be. Rays of white light looked like an image of God I was familiar with from my Catholic childhood. The child in me trembled; the grown-up looked in awe. I walked down my steep street to the beach at two in the morning. Other people were there, standing on the sand, heads tilted upwards. I asked what was happening. Is it the end of the world? I heard that child's voice ask. It's the Southern Lights, they said. A real good one.

I asked a colleague the next day if he'd seen the Southern Lights last night. What channel? he said.

Have you ever seen the Lights? wrote Ralph. Down here, it's really common. It displays for a lot of nights in a row.

There were many details we didn't know about each other, a lot of questions we never had time to ask.

The second time was on a bus going north from Hobart. The driver turned off the interior bus lights so the red glow in the sky was apparent. Like a tour guide he said, On the left you'll see the Southern Lights. The whaddayacallit? Does anyone know its botanical name? University student couples going home for the weekend snickered under their blankets.

I get up early to go down to the beach before anyone else is there. It is not like Australia where people are jogging or walking the dog at this hour. Sun worship is still devoted here, especially when the sun is high in the sky, and hot, and dangerous. Now the sun is just up and there is a golden milkiness about the sea. A small plane flies overhead and dips a wing. I wave, not knowing whether it is Don or not.

The third time I saw it was after you left. I was staying at a friend's house while I looked for a new one of my own. Our house was too big without you – all I could feel was the space around me. I was sleeping in my friend's square sun room which had large windows on three sides, composed of small panes of glass. The light in the sky woke me and I lay staring at the pulsing white brightness, surrounded by it, pinned down by it, in it. It played for hours and when it finally subsided I got up and sat at the window letting the dark seep back into me, comfortingly.

I thought I could tell you about it when you came back. But you didn't.

In ancient times the aurora was thought to be an omen of disaster.

I clean my lenses and prepare them for my trip to the village where Grazia Deledda lived. I will attempt to see places through her eyes.

Carita is having a night off and a girl from the town is waiting on tables. The little terrace is full already and it's just dusk.

At our table we have champagne. It is Carita's birthday. She is fifty-three and radiant. Her elegant indigo suit is patterned with Egyptian profiled figures. She lifts a strand of hair to wind in at the back of her head and proposes a toast.

May we have happiness in our lives. Or, even better, vision.

We clink glasses and drink. The champagne is cold and delicious and we are all in good spirits. I have taken my first lot of photographs. The colours in the village bled into one another in the soft light of the afternoon as if the world had no edges, as though it were all of a piece. I know the photographs will be good.

Colours, said Goethe, are the deeds and sufferings of light.

⁂

Today I am not happy with the light in the village. I mooch about in shadows and sit under dull awnings. I determine to get something useful from the day and turn my viewfinder on the square, the cafés, the people. Across from me, away across the cobblestone square, a couple lean into each other to kiss. I zoom in and click the shutter before I recognise them. The mechanical clatter hangs in the air around my head. I lower the camera and don't look again. I sit back. I feel disbelief, belief, disbelief. I order wine and the waiter jokes that the wine is young and green, like me. I pull my mouth, my face, to humour him, but he sees his failure, shrugs a shrug that involves his whole upper body and leaves me to mutter to myself.

I am witness, reluctant voyeur. I wonder what will happen. I wonder how to behave. I am shocked and, yes, ridiculous as it is, somehow feel that it is I who have been betrayed.

Carita notices the change in me and says, Ah, I see now what has happened. You have recreated events according to your own lights. You are a photographer. Surely you understand how many alterations you can make to the way something is seen. You do not see the thing itself; you see yourself. Yes. Do not presume to judge what you do not understand. These are our lives, and you are visiting them. You can walk away.

Watching them together I realise that seeing is not understanding and that photographs will not tell me what it is I want to know.

September 30th

Today I accepted Don's offer. We will fly up to meet tomorrow's sunrise. I will leave my camera in my room.

Blood harvest

She hangs her slipshod beauty over the ship's stern rail and all those gathered on the rear deck, economy class, to see the sun set, watch her from the corners of their eyes. She lifts her elastic-sided boots from the riveted red deck metal and points them straight behind her. She lifts her arms, spreads them in front of her, and the six inch wide metal top of the deck rail cutting into her belly is all that holds her aloft. She stretches there like a gliding eagle above the ravelling wake water, which is dark as blood in the labouring sunlight. Merely watching her, one has a sense of flying backwards – the horizon, the world, churning backwards beneath her bird's eye view.

How pretentious, some think. Wants attention, others whisper, nudging. But Madeleine hovers in her eyrie, oblivious. To me, she is majestic, doing what I would never dream of doing, even if I were alone. And yet I know it is exactly what I want, to hang there above the heel-lifting draught of air and water and to be utterly myself.

We don't meet until the ferry docks in Heraklion. It is an accident, a thong of her leather hold-all entangling with a strap of my nylon backpack as we walk the plank to shore. As we detach our worldly belongings, we introduce ourselves. Not as Madeleine who soars above boat wakes, or Katy who tries to make herself invisible, but as Madeleine from Prince Edward Island and Katy from New South Wales. What kind of whales? Madeleine asks. New South? Is that like Southern Right? Like Humpback? We laugh a little but then she takes me by the hand and says, Let me take you somewhere they serve free olives with each ouzo. I, who have never been singled out before in my life, have been taken under the wing of an angel, someone who flies in the face of expectation.

We manage five chalky ouzos and all the accompanying green olives before we hitch a ride in a ute to Chania. On the way the driver, who must be older than my father and is as bald, takes out his withered weenie and tries to make it point at the steering wheel the way the knobbed gear stick does in third. Madeleine nudges me but as I look across he puts it away. When he drops us outside the town, she says, Thanks, gramps, nice try.

We find a room for three dollars a night, three of *my* dollars. It is above a dry-cleaning shop and a shop which sells plates glazed in colours of the islands, blue and white and celadon green. The room is beautiful. Twenty-five feet by fifteen of magenta terrazzo. Empty but for a sink with a cold tap above a rust-red stain, and two single iron beds. Full length French doors opening out over the street above the plate seller's shop. Flaking blue-painted shutters the length of the French doors. We close the shutters and lie on the silky terrazzo in striated sunlight. It is like floating in a cold river.

How long have you been away? I ask, hating myself for banality.

Three years, Madeleine says. Give or take a month or two.

Don't you get homesick? Hating myself for the need to banish silence.

What? Miss my family? She laughs. Listen. I've got a mother who thinks she alone shouldn't age past thirty-five and spends most of her time working on ways to look like she hasn't. And then I've got a father who acts like he *is* thirty-five and lives with a woman who actually is. They divorced when I was eleven. I went to boarding school from then on. And in school holidays I went to camp. Riding camp. Swimming camp. Athletics camp. Hiking camp. I learned all kinds of useful things. I learned how to trap unwary animals and skin them with my Swiss Army knife. I learned to be self sufficient. I learned to use whatever is to hand. I learned to survive.

Her leather hold-all is the colour of south-east Australian sand. It feels as soft as a grandmother's skin when kissed after many years. She tells me she retrieved it from a rubbish skip and gave it some tender loving care. It is the kind of bag a governess would once have brought to the front step of a new position saying her luggage was on its way, whether it was or not. There is little in it. Madeleine seems to need nothing. Even her boots, her out-of-season shorts and her shirt are the merest genuflection in the direction of convention. She could as easily go naked. Her hair is coarsely stranded like a horse's mane. I feel I could count each strand, given time. She is like a filly, or a colt, perfect, energetic, self-sufficient, impatient. When I say this to her much later, she laughs. More like a zebra perhaps, she says. Something bizarre. An oddball animal. But I think of a zebra, crazily beautiful, carelessly so, and I think she is right.

We have come to pick oranges – at least I have. But there is still snow on the mountains and we spend days simply watching it melt in the growing warmth of the sunshine. Or traipsing through the covered market. Or sitting in a café. Others are drawn to Madeleine but she shuns them and I am secretly delighted. The light of her attention shines only on me.

We buy whatever is cheapest. This is how Madeleine has survived for so long on so little. In Israel she lived on avocados and figs; in France, couscous; in Italy, slices of pizza left over in streetside shops. In our room we eat tomatoes and fetta cheese and we drink ouzo and retsina. We walk by the old port through pools of yellow light thrown by lamps outside empty tavernas.

She is drawn to islands. The smaller the better. Crete is too big but that was the ferry she'd wound up on. We are all islands, she tells me.

Don't you know the poem? I ask, knowing it is the wrong thing. No man is an island.

She shrugs and repeats, We are all islands.

We have heard there is a village along the coast with the best yoghurt in all of Crete. In watery sunshine we set off, not by road, but on a faint track hugging the water. She talks at the air and I hurry to stay close enough to catch each flung word.

The year I turned thirteen I went to swimming camp for the first time. Every day we walked to what they called The Lake. It was really a tepid pond. There was a beautiful dark girl called Francesca. They used to do buddy calls – blow the whistle and everyone checks on their buddy. Francesca was my buddy. Whenever the whistle blew and I looked for her she was floating face down in the murky water. I'd race to grab her, my heart in my mouth. She'd taught herself to do deadman's float and was practising it. I told her not to. The counsellors told her not to. But she did it anyway. She'd stand up and take a big gulp of air and look pleased with herself for staying down so long. After a while I stopped rushing over. One time they whistled and I didn't even look. Not until the shouting started. That time she wasn't pretending.

I thought I'd never go back to that camp but it was cheap and my mother had been overspending on skintucks. She sent me again the next year. The first day we walked to the pond, a car stopped right beside me and this boy – beautiful he was, like a movie star – leaned out and said, Care for a spin, camper? I hopped in and that night I rang the camp and told them if they said nothing about it to anyone, I'd be back on the Friday ready for my mother to pick me up on the Saturday. Otherwise, blame for my abduction would undoubtedly fall on them. They couldn't risk another scandal. I don't know what they told the other happy campers. I went back. My mother picked me up. No one was any the wiser. I realised then that you can usually do exactly what you like.

I puff from trying to keep up with her. She suddenly says, Let's take a break here. She lies down on some rocks and takes off her shirt to catch the weak sun. Her nipples look like calves' horn mounds beginning to show. Her breasts are the same brown all over. I take off my T-shirt and lie back as if I do this sort of thing all the time. Nice white swimsuit, Madeleine teases, and tickles my nipples until I have to run away.

There is a café where contractors come to find pickers. I go there and sit with other hopefuls for two mornings. Madeleine stays in bed saying she will join me one of these days. On the third morning I am chosen along with an Australian boy with long blond hair. He nods to me as if we don't speak the same language, don't come from the same country, but I know just by looking. The contractor calls him Yannis. We bump along in the back of the contractor's truck, stopping to pick up three Greek women, two of them with young sons in tow. We are driven to an orchard where crates lie higgledy-piggledy under trees. Ladders lean against trunks. With gestures and single Greek words we are shown what to do.

Yannis and I are to be partners, like it or not. We still don't speak. We continue the language of hand and head movement. Soon I have picked up Greek words for crate, ladder, lunchtime, tired. I use them with Yannis and he understands. At lunchtime, the Greek women overturn crates, fling a cloth, conjure cheese, bread, olives, wine. We feast in cold green air among orange trees. In the afternoon, languor streams in my blood. I long to nap. I loll at the top of my ladder but my hands continue picking fast. If I don't pick enough I won't be chosen tomorrow.

Next morning the contractor points to me again and I jump in the truck with Yannis. We nod hello. I point questioningly to the other drifters hunched over coffees inside the café. Yannis lifts two fingers to his lips and pretends to inhale deeply, closing his eyes. That explains the slowness. The contractor picks it easily enough. Too slow for his fast-ripening oranges.

Madeleine still doesn't get out of bed in time. On the fourth day she is in the café waiting when I return. She has the slowness in her eyes. I take her home. I pull ten oranges from my bag. I tell her what happened. After lunch I asked the women if I might eat an orange. They could not control their laughter. Yes, yes, of course, of course, they said and laughed more. Four days, and it had not occurred to me to eat an orange. I peeled the skin away with hands crosshatched by orange tree spikes. I parted the segments and pulled open the flesh. The juice ran red, like red currant syrup. I looked up at the others. Blood oranges, said the Australian boy.

I begin to bring oranges home every evening and Madeleine turns them into delights. Iced red juice with yellow curling lemon peel and green mint sprigs. Hot blood orange sugar syrup over golden pancakes. Blood orange, red pepper and chilli salsa with salty grilled sardines. We wash everything down with retsina and the slowness goes out of her eyes. I give her money from picking to buy things from the market but still she transforms blood oranges into our meals, our drinks, our livelihood.

After twenty nights in the airy room there is a new snowfall on the mountains and Madeleine comes into my bed to keep warm. I smell blood oranges on her breath and when she touches my face with her hand it is as if I am again on the ladder among oranges. Her breath blankets my skin and melts limbs stiff and awkward with newness. When I try to stop her mouth she says, It's all right.

On Sunday we go to the market. Arm in arm. Hand in hand. Shame, call out some Greek boys. We smile at them. A little further on Madeleine lifts up her shirt and turns to show them her breasts. They are startled, like young deer. Madeleine laughs and kisses me on the mouth right in front of a gaping stall-holder behind a perfect pyramid of blood oranges.

Madeleine is deft with her Swiss Army knife. She peels waxy rind from an orange into a spiralling mobile hung between thumb and forefinger. One day when I come back from the orchard, orange peel is strung out across the terrazzo in primitive lettering spelling, Madeleine loves Katy.

Madeleine gets up earlier as the days become warmer. She squeezes fresh blood red juice for both of us. She comes to the café with me, but she is never chosen for the orchards. She gets the slow look in her eyes again. Sometimes her lips and her tongue are slow. I try to quicken them with mine. She laughs. She merely shrugs when she is passed over at the café, and blows a kiss to where I crouch in the back of the truck. Then she settles back in her chair among the growing number of travellers. I catch Yannis looking at me thoughtfully.

On Wednesday of the last week of picking, our contractor collects us as usual. The truck bounces and sways further and further away from Chania and Yannis and I look at each other with surprise. We have not stopped for the women. We roll into the yard of a farmhouse and the two Greek boys who pick with us come running out. Behind them come the women. One of them indicates this is her home and we are welcome.

We go inside and find a table laden with food, more than seems possible in such a small room. Bottles are produced and opened and we are clinking glasses and toasting and eating and laughing without having any idea what is going on. Someone points to a faded picture of a saint on the wall and we decide it must be a holy day. We relax and enjoy ourselves. Yannis tells me he is from Sydney. He is afraid of meeting only other Australians, worse still, Sydneysiders. We clink glasses and use all the Greek words we know with each other and our hosts. We are given the tidbits, eyeballs of fish, testes of lamb. The two boys take us by the hand and lead us out of the house. We go across the yard to a small field where two goats are tethered. The boys kneel and milk a goat each and present us with glasses of warm cheesy-smelling milk. Back in the house we eat baklava and halva. Finally we are loaded up with leftovers. No blood oranges today. It is dark when we climb into the back of the truck. I worry for a moment about Madeleine but then fall asleep despite the rough ride. When I wake, Yannis has put his arm around me to cushion the bumps.

There is only a low lamplight between cracks in the shutters as I approach our room from the street. I realise it is the first time I have seen the room from outside at night without Madeleine. I climb the stairs quietly, thinking she will be asleep, imagining her form in the bed, arms flung across pillows.

It takes only a second to know she is not there. I absorb the silence of the room, the empty bed, the complete lack of breath and life. I realise instantly that she is not in the bathroom or down at the café or off in some bar. She is gone. I am already missing her as I take in the absence of her clothes and few possessions, the soft honey-coloured tote bag. It probably took only minutes to pick up her life and move on.

I walk to the rumpled bed. The pillows are cold. For a moment I think that the small red stain on the sheet is blood orange juice but, when I lower my head and breathe in, it has the bitter-edged soft scent of blood. It is already almost dry.

All night as I toss and try to sleep I am aware of that darkening patch of red beneath me. It is a puzzle, her only note, and I am at a loss to read it.

Now, as the mass of Prince Edward Island takes on definition ahead of the ship, I turn and look backwards. I have stood here on the rear deck remembering, not noticing wind whipping my clothes and hair. The grey sea is garlanded with white. I walk towards the stern railing and look down the path of wake, widening then disappearing. The sensation is as much one of travelling forwards as backwards, or both at once. The metal is cold against my stomach. I feel my heels lift in anticipation.

Sojourn

Robert has drunk too much brandy trying to dull the pain in his tooth, so we stop the Land Rover in a village square and look for a likely bar. The waiter waves us inside but we want to sit outside at one of the round wrought-iron tables and he throws his hands in the air.

We keep an eye on the Land Rover because it is loaded with our worldly possessions. Gas bottles are lined up along one side of the roof rack and a windsurfer mast points over the bonnet. The back is a chaos of awkward objects carefully covered with blankets and cushions so we may still climb in and sleep. Surprisingly, we sleep soundly every night, tucked into each other, dreaming separate dreams of what we will make of our lives. In the mornings we wake bemused to landscapes unknown except for those of each other's body and temperament, topography we could map with great precision.

The throbbing in Robert's tooth will not let up. He throws back one Pernod after another. His eyes are looking wild, as if they are filling up with seawater; his hair is dishevelled and he rubs his hands through it roughly as though to scrape away the pain in his skull.

We roll cigarettes and order more drinks. The waiter has thawed now he sees we are good customers. He talks windsurfing to Robert and I interpret. I explain about the tooth and he disappears into the bar, returning with two white tablets in the palm of his hand. Robert swallows them unquestioningly, beyond caring. But I know part of him is enjoying this, the trial of it, the test of his endurance.

The waiter, Alain, says what a pity it's Saturday night or he could take us to a good dentist. Yes, what a pity, we nod. But that would be too easy.

The square livens up as darkness sneaks among the trees and lights come on. Couples stroll and join us at outside tables. Groups of young men in leather jackets arrive and disappear inside. Two girls drive up in one of those tiny Renaults that look as if they've been built from an old pedal car and a forty-four gallon drum. They are dressed to kill in short skirts, long boots, and tops which cling to their breasts. Men put glasses to lips and watch from lowered eyes as the girls saunter across the terrace into the bar.

Robert does not want to eat. He is a mummy wrapped in a shroud of brandy and Pernod. Despite the pain, he has driven all day, not trusting the old Land Rover's idiosyncrasies to my hands. He is determined to get back to England to see a dentist.

We usually take back roads and meander. We stop at vineyards to taste and buy wine. We stop in fields where poppies of madder red grow in profusion and throw down our blanket, drink the wine, eat food bought in the last village, make love. Once, lying naked together in the sun, we were startled by a train's rattle and roar and looked up in time to see driver and mate waving from the engine platform. The train whistled a long hoot that rang in our ears for an hour. But these last two days we have taken highways, trundling along with traffic overtaking us, the Land Rover vibrating and rattling and the engine growling so that we can't hear each other above the din. What was meant to be a lingering journey has turned into a headlong rush.

Robert goes to the Land Rover for more tobacco and comes back looking wilder than ever. I still get the urge when I see him to climb up onto his powerful body and hang there like a small animal; he is like a tree and I seek its refuge. No one has held me in an embrace all through the night the way he has, quieted my body as he has. I am enveloped still by his physical presence, but no longer by his love.

We've got a flat tyre, he says, then adds, And no spare.

In some ways it doesn't matter at all, nothing does. We could sit here at this bar until something changes; we could do nothing, not act, and then we wouldn't be responsible for anything that happens.

We hum over possibilities and decide on temporary inaction and sleeping in the Land Rover right where it is, under the plane trees in the middle of the town square. If we are discreet, the gendarmes won't bother us. Alain says he will think of something.

When we were packing, I came across a letter Robert had written to me in early days. I read,

Are we travelling this journey together or are you my journey and I yours? Are we landscapes that remain in the mind like photographs? I love to journey through your landscape. I love its contours. Let me lie by your streams so that the flow lulls me. Let me climb your mountains and run along your beaches so that it exhilarates me. Let me trek through your muddy lowlands so that it exhausts me. Let me gaze over your ocean so that it inspires me and swim in it so that it liberates me. I invite you to explore the landscape of me. Some of it is tamed, some of it is wilderness. You may find yourself lost. Remember, the journey is all.

I was rocked by this letter, mainly because I hadn't remembered it. I thought the landscape metaphor was mine. Robert doesn't write often; I know what this must have cost him. There are spelling mistakes. It comes from the heart.

I'm the writer. When is the last time I wrote him a love letter?

Bicycle bells and calls of *Bonjour* wake us and we forego our early morning lovemaking thinking it's too public. We both know it is owing. We are not out of love with intimacy of this kind. Robert says the pain has eased, but his head aches from drinking. I must look a sight. I pull on tights and a windcheater and climb into the front seat, turning the rear-view mirror down to see. It is too close. I clamber out into the cool bright air and comb my hair using my reflection in the window. I look a bit more respectable but, after all, I have spent the night in the arms of an unshaven man with Pernod and tobacco on his breath and the nozzle of a scuba-diving tank in the small of my back.

From the patisserie I bring back a pastry each and Robert gets coffees from Alain who is already sweeping the terrace and wiping down tables. We sit close together on a bench under plane trees to eat our breakfast. Two or three leaves drift down to lie on the cobbles next to the back passenger side tyre which is flat as flat, the rim bending rubber out to reveal dry fissures. With all the weight in the back we know it isn't doing the tyre any good. The coffee helps me begin to think about the problem. Robert already has the solution.

There are small canisters to be bought from general stores which are instant but temporary puncture repair kits. I can't believe such things exist but Robert knows about objects, practicalities. Alain offers to drive us. When he shows up, after help has arrived for the bar, he is driving the Renault the two girls arrived in last night.

I go along, not because I am needed to make the purchase but because Alain and Robert can talk to each other through me.

Robert inserts the canister nozzle and presses. The Land Rover lifts from its dropped-hip pose, like an elephant waking up. It goes up only so far and stops. We shake hands with Alain and thank him. We leap into the cab and drive like maniacs to a garage only to find they don't have an air pressure hose. We drive till we find another garage. They have one but they don't turn it on for Sundays. No, there is no other garage in this village but, of course, Monsieur, the next village has one. It is still early. We hurtle out of the straggling village and into vivid green pastures, my head out the window, eyes on the tyre. It's getting flatter. Soon the flap, flap, flap is unbearable and we pull over onto the narrow verge. The sun is getting hot now. I long for a bath, a shower, a swim. We sit on warm grass and look for inspiration.

It is me who thinks of the diving tanks and the repair kit from the inflatable dinghy. We can patch the tube and inflate the tyre from the tanks. Robert kisses me and tells me that I'm brilliant. I feel brilliant. It is Robert who is good at innovative solutions. The only problems will be getting the tyre off the rim and the air out of the tank and into the tube.

We work on the tyre for some time, levering and pulling till sweat is running into our eyes and our fingers ache. Finally it is off, inner tube exposed like a large intestine. Robert locates the puncture and works on the patch while I sit in shade. Swearing loudly, we get the tyre back on the rim. Robert sits and thinks. A car pulls up and two French lads get out to ask what's happening. They shake their heads when I explain our plan. They sit down with Robert and ponder the two diving tanks and various odds and ends from which he is attempting to make a valve. They say, Better to wait till tomorrow and get a new tube. They don't know about the tooth. They tear off again, their exhaust fumes hanging in the hot sunshine.

Robert has fashioned a valve. I don't know how. He is all smiles. We put the tyre back on the Land Rover and turn on the tank's air pressure. The tyre fattens and we jump up and down and hug.

A brown river snakes through overhanging trees,

undercutting rich reddish purple soil. Fishermen stand in the shallows in waders up to their thighs. We are dirty and sweaty and my hands ache from manipulating the tyre. I long to get into the river.

Turning a bend in the road we drive into a village which seems to consist only of a square and the buildings around it. Shutters are down. Heat shimmers off bitumen. The sun is high overhead. We see no one but when we drive around the square the stammer of a television blares out from a bar. We stop. The tyre looks fine. We go into the bar to buy a bottle of drinking water.

In the cool interior, cigarette smoke curls up by the ear of a woman with dyed red hair who is sitting alone at one of the four tables. Her eyes do not swerve from the television on a bracketed shelf high on the wall. I say what we want and she says, *Oui*, and somehow swivels out of her chair and moves behind the bar, her eyes never leaving the television. I turn to look at what she is watching. On the screen, a man in a car calls a girl over to ask directions. He has a map spread out on his lap. The girl leans into the car and the man winds up the window, jamming her neck. The man gets out of the passenger door, goes around to the driver's side, pulls up the girl's dress and rapes her.

When the bar woman asks for money, I ask Robert to pay her and I go outside. The heat is making me dizzy.

The tyre is still fine. We drive down a deserted lane to the river, walk gingerly in bare feet over the round hot stones till we find a deep pool. We take off our clothes. I let the water soothe me. I swim below the surface where sunlight reflects from suspended particles. Small fish dart away. I've brought shampoo and I wash my hair, use the lather to wash my body. Robert, as always when we are in water together, wants to fuck. I swim away from him and float on my back, keeping my mind on blue cloudless sky.

As we dry on the smooth stones, sun on skin does its work. A tickle of breeze raises goose bumps and the hair along our arms. I move into Robert's side and we kiss hard and long, pretending that's all we might do, until the desperation in the rest of our bodies is unbearable. With river water like dew on my skin, I am a ripe, early-morning peach. Robert slits me open to find the stone. He pushes himself into me and I rise up under his chest.

When eventually we ease apart, we see a man with a little black dog turning away from the river bank.

We get back into the water and play. We let well-being fill us. When we are like this together, Robert is happy and I suppose I am, too.

Back at the Land Rover, we find the tyre has gone flat again. Better to wait till tomorrow, I say. But Robert wants to push on. He reminds me of his tooth and I realise, guiltily, I had forgotten.

The whole process is repeated. The patches meant for the dinghy are not strong enough for the pressure of an inner tube but we do it all again anyway and push north. We cover some miles, driving on back roads through green fields and market gardens. The tyre begins to flap and we look for a place where we can get off the road. We stop where a lane turns off to a cluster of houses and where there is a patch of grass under some trees. We get out to look. The rim is on the ground again. I spread my hands out; my knuckles are bruised and scraped from jamming between the tyre and the rim. I say I don't want to try again.

A man comes by, from a nearby house, and when I explain our plight he offers to take us into town in the morning, to a garage where we can have a new tube put in the tyre.

In the back of the Land Rover, I uncover a big round tin of sardines which has been with us since we left the coast. I pick up an empty water bottle, some money, and tell Robert I am going to the farmhouse further down the road to see if I can get water and bread.

The farmhouse is typically large and plain and quite beautiful, a contrast to the bungalows near where the Land Rover is parked. The yellow gravel driveway is neatly kept as are the fields on either side. Geese and ducks scatter noisily as I walk into the farmyard.

An old man and woman stand together in the open doorway at the side of the house as if waiting for me, their arms linked at the elbow. I smile and practise in my head what I will say. We stand on the threshold of the house, and their faces and hands come alive as I tell my story. They catch their breath; they laugh out loud. Their hands flutter in the air, slap their foreheads, cover their mouths. In the end they stand aside and ask me into the kitchen. It is the most pleasing room I have ever seen – high bare walls, flagstone floor, a large wooden table in the centre, a huge kitchen range and a dresser.

The man fills up my water bottle and cuts off half a big crusty round loaf of bread. The woman has disappeared and now returns with a bottle of red wine. I offer my money but they laugh and close my hands and push me out the door into the fading sunlight.

Kafka's house

I wait under the clock-tower at ten to five. I scan passers-by but you aren't among them. We were last here twelve years ago. We said we would meet again in ten years' time, but life is never so neat.

There are no beautiful clock towers where I am from, no campaniles to guide lost wanderers or to position lovers so one can find them with ease; there are freeways, shopping malls and telephone booths. This clock bears fifteenth century figures and a narrative of life and death and faith. Faith. Something this country has had to be good at. On the hour, the square will fill with people come to watch the antique movement of the clock. Death will appear and upend his hourglass; twelve apostles will pass by and nod to onlookers; a cock will crow and the hour will chime. One. Two. Three. Four. Five.

Three days now I have waited as I said I would, at five o'clock, off to one side so that I need not look directly into the faces of clock watchers. O'clock, of the clock, we are all of the clock; it rules us mercilessly but we comply, we allow its sovereignty, and our anxiety is infinite.

I am disappointed you have not turned up. So much of the new Prague has offered itself, the same way the city originally opened to us when we were lovers here. I long to share the rediscovery with you. But in our letters we could not manage to make an arrangement more exact than this. We would try, we said. Perhaps a secret part of us enjoyed the uncertainty, the open-endedness, the small question mark in our very certain lives. I understand that you are busy, in demand. A festival in Belgium, a meeting with your publisher in Paris. I wrote to say I would wait at five each evening beneath the clock. That's what I intend to do.

Charles Bridge is much the same as it was twelve years ago. Artists and buskers still converge among statues, and the Vltava flows undaunted by history beneath the stone. I can still have my portrait painted, my fortune told, my hair braided, or my photo taken with a five-foot snake draped along my shoulders like a stole. I can still buy souvenirs, trinkets, silver jewellery, prints, paintings, or a little escape from reality.

I stand listening to middle European folk songs, Gypsy melodies, songs in English. This used to be our milieu – this itinerant, carefree, sun-tanned, polyglot crowd who move easily into the spaces between things.

I can't be as free as that any more. I would feel the risk too acutely. They take their lives in their hands at every turn, oblivious to it, living without counting the cost. It bothers me, though, my loss of abandon, my careful clinging to life in this way, my wanting to make a safe place to dwell. I don't know if it is simply a matter of getting older, or of being a mother, or the sense of mortality, a recognition of the preciousness of each moment, each hour. And the fact that there is so much to do. So much to write. I feel the tension. Something is lost in trying to hold on, and what if it is the very thing you needed to hold on to?

I have your portrait on my bedroom wall. Remember the Mauritian woman who sang in French while she painted you? I wonder how twelve years will have changed you?

Lovers kiss and lean over the side of the bridge watching the water flow fast, dizzyingly, feeling the suck of it, feeling their heels grow light. I look at the brown water, and at the lovers, trying not to see how hands move over hair and skin, hips jutting and meeting through thin summer clothes. I try not to see, and I try to see. The pain of it is poignant and seductive. I feel desire, hot like the sun on my hair.

On the castle side of the river a film crew is setting up on the bank beneath the tower. A crowd has gathered to watch the action; everybody seems to have all the time in the world. As if there were no clocks.

I walk across the bridge.

The castle. This has been my excuse. To return to Kafka's city. To write about writers who wrote about the deep issues of existence. The awful thing is needing an excuse at all.

We lived a floating life back then. No ties, no responsibilities. At the same time we craved permanence, love. Part of us was tired of always seeking, moving on. We were preparing to slough off that skin of youthful adventure, but were attached to it still, the only skin we knew; we were snug in its contours. We weren't quite ready for a new skin. We couldn't imagine it.

Ah, your skin.

I wonder where you are right now. On a train hurtling towards Prague, tired from the journey and fitful sleep? Waiting at the airport in Paris? Arriving?

The room I have taken is large and beautiful. It reminds me of the room we shared here last time, only it is ten times more expensive. It is in a stone building up the hill from the National Museum. It was in front of the museum that the student, Jan Palach, set fire to himself to express his opposition to the '68 invasion, to show his seriousness. Remember all the wreaths we had to skirt around when we climbed the steps? The wooden street door to the apartment block is thick and heavy. I push it open and enter the cool dimness. I unlock the apartment door with the key I have been given. My room looks out onto an internal square, quiet and green and cool. Sometimes elderly men and women sit there together, hands resting on walking sticks, and I yearn to know what it is they say as they lean towards each other. I close the shutters against the light, and rest.

The bathroom is a curtained-off space in the kitchen and it is usually when I make my way to the bathroom that I encounter my hosts. I say *Dobry den* and *Nashledanou* but I have only a few coins of this strange language to spend. We switch to French. Monsieur asks, *Elle est arrivée?* No, I say, she hasn't arrived. Not yet. Maybe tomorrow. She will be happy, I say, to have a room as beautiful and spacious as this waiting for her. The things we can talk about are determined by my limited French. It could not express the issues I would like to discuss. For example, Were you, Monsieur, a part of the people's movement which finally toppled the old order? Did you see it coming? Had anyone foreseen it, written about it?

It was ordinary people, fed up with oppression, who rose up and resisted. The power of that idea fills my mind. So many times the resistance must have been close to achieving the overthrow, but no, it took the right time, a readiness, all the pieces being in place. But in the end, that is what it took – people like Monsieur saying, Enough! Why, then, do we feel so helpless? At the airport, leaving Australia, I had noticed an Amnesty International poster with the slogan, USE the freedom!

In the evening I hear the unsteady clack clack clack of a typewriter from some room in the house. Is Monsieur a writer, a journalist, or simply a good correspondent? Perhaps he participated in *samizdat*. It was a time when writing was feared. And for good reason. Writing is feared when there are things to hide.

This morning, I am off to visit the house on Kaprova Street where Franz Kafka was born. I want to see if there are any clues. How do you go about writing a novel which expresses the state of man and the state of society? Before coming to Europe I attended a writers' festival at which a historian declared the Australian novel politically impotent, saying that it is in history and non-fiction books people now seek enlightenment about our past and our present. I refuse to accept this. But where is the Australian equivalent of *The Trial* or *The Castle*?

There aren't any clues, though, only some faded photographs in a quaint conjoined lodging on a narrow laneway near Old Town Square. Kafka later lived in similar homes close by. Someone once said of Kafka that, had he lived in a real house instead of cramped crowded quarters, he would never have written his visionary works, that he may not have written anything at all.

Today there is a wedding in the church of St Nicolas. The bride and groom cross the square to stand beneath the astronomical clock for photos. They smile and wave as if they are celebrities. The gathered tourists reinforce this illusion and take photos of the couple as well as of the astronomical clock. We are both married now. At least you are. I *was*. It was a failure. In writing circles we say failure is inevitable on the road to success. Is it the same with marriage, do you think? You haven't said yours is a failure. You don't say much about it at all, which is, I suppose, why I have my suspicions. I'm reading between the lines. Some things are only ever told face to face.

When we were last here, the split between the Czech Republic and Slovakia was announced. Not a trial separation – a divorce. We were in Bratislava at the time Meciar made the announcement. Citizens gathered in the town square and applauded quietly. We expected a festive atmosphere, fireworks. That night people strolled demurely by the Danube as usual, perhaps a little more subdued if anything. Were they thinking, More change! or What now? Perhaps they were wondering if this would lead to another failure.

Perhaps they missed their chains and were finding the new freedom a fearful thing.

We both became writers. You were already writing when I knew you then, poetry mainly, but afterwards you branched out, blossomed. You've become famous. You said it was the only way to hold on to your freedom after you were married. You could disappear into your books and come back only when you felt like it. I was slower to start, but you gave me inspiration. You tell me your books are now found in airports in Germany and supermarkets in Scandinavia. Not bad for a Canadian housewife, you say. Now that the money has given you security and independence, I wonder if you'll move on to something less lightweight. We used to say money is only valuable in that it allows you the freedom to do what you really want to do. But new directions mean new possibilities for failure.

I've stuck to short stories and magazine articles. This trip will provide material for an article in one of the weekend magazines. In my heart, I want to write something substantial, something challenging and lasting, but how to begin, how to choose a story to carry your passions, ideas, convictions? Brett Whiteley said he could have painted every single thing around him and that selecting a subject for attention is a moral choice.

Kafka published only short stories in his lifetime. He wanted his other manuscripts burned after he died. But his friend Max Brod ignored the request, edited and published Kafka's novels. Imagine that – you write what turns out to be great novels of our time but you never know it.

Remember, on that last night, we went out to an Italian restaurant near the Jewish Quarter cemetery, and drank a bottle of German wine. The waiter said he was from near Banska Bystrica and would now return home. He said with a sigh that Prague would no longer be a good place for people like him. He said that Europe is not kind to minorities. He said his people's stories are seldom told.

Afterwards we went with the flow of the evening crowd in the narrow streets, drawn inevitably to the bridge. We strolled across. Young people were wearing long thin bands of fluorescent light – green, orange, yellow – around their necks or wrists or whipping them through the air leaving trails, waves, arcs of light, suspended for a second on nothing. We found the seller. He had circles of coloured light in his hair, about his ankles, dangling from his ears. We bought two of the tubes and snapped them to release the fluid and the glow. We said, We are glow worms! We are magicians!

When we leaned over the side of the bridge, we saw the spangles among restaurant lights below, and saw them bobbing along streets fanning out from the bridge. Today's gimmick, we said. But waved the sticks like wands.

I stand further off to the side this time as the clock begins its story. I stand away from the hubbub and flashes of cameras, and that is how I see you before you see me, your blond hair still in waves like a forties' movie star. I suddenly remember that you've always said you hate being glamorous, that it gives people the wrong impression.

We sit at a café in Old Town Square, talk and giggle like the young women we were when we sat here last. We collect your suitcase from the station and take a bus to the museum, then walk out of Wenceslas Square and up the street. I am looking forward to showing you our room.

Monsieur comes out into the hallway when I call.

Ah, elle est arrivée, he says.

Yes. She is here.

How much sugar?

I think about the word 'rather' as I drive home through empty, wet streets, white lines gone under oily sheen. I'd rather. This rather than that. Oh, rather, as the English say. I rather think I will. Rather rather rather. What a weird word it's become. It turns non-sensical on the top of my tongue and I want to spit it out. I knew a word for this once. Briefly. A word for the phenomenon of words losing meaning through repetition. (Why does it happen? Is that how tenuous our grasp of reality is?) Trouble is, once I'd heard it, I said it over and over and it lost its meaning and I forgot it. I've never recovered it. I ask likely people from time to time, professors, linguists, philosophers. No joy. I think about how I might look it up in *Roget's*, what section of experience I would find it in. I think about how staggering it was when I realised what a thesaurus does, carves up reality, unreality, experience, everything into chunks. I think about Roget himself and those years in prison. How full his brain must have been.

What I would think of to do if I had endless prison days ahead. Something useful. I think about usefulness, and why we crave it. Why not be satisfied with a completely useless life, nothing gained, nor learned, nor given? Of what use am I? I drive four blocks while I mull that one over. Well, I teach. But I do not decide whether what I teach is useful. That is assumed.

Don't you notice the way this happens – you think something, one thought leads to another and before you know it you've driven right past your street, your mind describing wiper arcs, suspended in the pellets of rain in the light, driving an old route all the way along the river and right to your door. Your lights are on. Stained glass – green, amber, blue – glows like a kaleidoscope, inviting. I turn the ignition off and gather my bearings out of reverie. I am in your driveway. I didn't choose to. I just. The rain. Wet. I was dreaming. Wet dreaming. Drive dreaming. It was bound to happen. A large well-travelled neural pathway has mapped the route to your house and this has jumped into the gap in mind activity. It's natural. But in front of me in the driveway is a small motorbike. I notice the way rain pings and pops off the plump metal. Whoever sits on that seat next will get a wet crotch. Speaking of which. This drive is out of bounds for this bike. This bike belongs to your past. Belongs to a woman from your past. Past. What's past is passed. Past,

past, past. Meaningless. It takes less and less time for the collapse of meaning to happen on my tongue. I spit pieces into the rain. Chips of words. Spit chips. You said. Never again. You said.

Sugar, I think. That's what I thought last time, so long ago, but I didn't have any and I didn't know what to do with it and anyway I didn't have the guts. Gutless wonder. I let you off the hook. Okay. You asked for it. Here we go. I look in the glove box. I find a hook, line and sinker, a champagne cork, two condoms (out of date), a flask of brandy with one mouthful in it (I drink it), two glowies, one paper clip, one screwdriver (Phillip's head), one Butter Menthol (I think), three packets of two sugar cubes and two sticks/tubes/long thin packets (no wonder no one learns the names of containers any more – what would you call those little clear plastic thingies of tomato sauce? There are two of those, too) of sugar. I don't take sugar. But I do buy coffee. I wonder how much it takes. I slip out of the car and rain instantly falls more heavily, drums, drowns out other sound, drenches me. I find the petrol cap (I suppose, it's round, shiny) take it off and drop all the sugar in. I drop one of the packets in for good measure.

When I look up you are standing on the porch, your silhouette against the stained glass. Your arms are folded. You don't look pleased to see me. What the fuck do you think you're doing, you yell above the rain. What does it look like, I yell back. Like you're sabotaging my bike, comes the reply. Your bike? *Your* bike? Ohmygodwhyhaveyouforsakenme? I stand in the driveway, my hair plastered over my eyes and I wonder why the rain is hot. Someone has turned the hot tap on. The drops roll down my face leaving hot tracks. They run off my chin and hit the wet mess of my clothes. You'd better come in out of the rain, you say. You don't sound all that angry. Not really.

How much sugar? you call out, and for a minute I panic. I'm not good at facing up to things. Especially things I've done myself. Then I realise what you mean. None, thanks, I call out in the direction of the kitchen. I've turned over a new leaf. I think I hear you say, That'll be the day, but I can't be sure. I imagine you getting down the mugs from the cupboards I painted yellow two summers ago, well yes, I started them, you finished them. For me the blue mug with fish on it and a hole where the handle joins, making it chatter when it's full. You come in with a tray and cups, fine china ones I've never seen before, the sort your mother leaves to you and you never know what to do with. Steam rises from the cups in swirling micro-climates. Nice cups, I say. Why does everything that comes from my mouth have to sound so smart-arsed? I think I even mean it but it doesn't sound that way. Just habit, I guess. Yes, they were Mum's, you say. I try to recall something about your mother. I'm hopeless on family stuff. I always think you've had enough of families by the time you leave home so why get involved with someone else's? When everybody gets together at Christmas, I stay home and read a good book. It's fantastic. So quiet. And I'll never get hit by a drunk-driver. Your Mum, I say inquiringly, trying to remember if I ever met her. Yes, my mother. You wouldn't remember her. I doubt you bothered to meet her, knowing you. Ouch, I say, but you continue, She died two months ago. Just like that. Diagnosed one week, gone the next. No time to ask all the things you want to ask, or say all the things you want to say. Like what? I ask, and you look at me in wonder. I realise I've skipped an important step, the condolence step, and I get out my sincerest voice, I am sorry, you must feel terrible. I can see you are placated.

It was always easy to placate you. I suppose I had a lot of practice, too. There was always something to be placating for. I don't mean to wind people up but it happens. You said I just didn't think about other people enough, that I didn't have a considerate bone in my body. Well, of course, I said. Hell is other people. Why would I want to think about them all the time? Well, what about me? you'd replied. How about thinking just about me, surely that's not too much to ask? That was towards the end. Before that, I suppose you thought I'd learn to be different. But I didn't. I was the same. I didn't want to be different than I was. Not even for you. Even though I loved you. Of course I loved you. I still love you. It wasn't me who pulled the plug, was it? I couldn't believe it the day you called it off. I thought you would handle it. But no, you said you loved me but you didn't know how to get in touch with me. I said I thought we had the touching part sorted out. Flippant to the end, that'd be right, you said. But I wasn't. I meant it. The way we made love was always wonderful. My pointy angles were smoothed down by our lovemaking and for hours afterwards I would feel like I thought people should feel all the time.

You are still talking about your mother but I have lost the thread. Do you believe in angels? I ask. Changing the subject is always a good ploy. You look at me carefully, suspiciously. Well, I didn't, but now . . . I butt in, They seem to be everywhere these days, don't they. You can do Adult Ed courses on getting in touch with your angels, freeing the angels, flying with the angels . . . You jerk up from your chair so suddenly that I stand up too, still holding my cup, and the blanket you gave me to wrap up in while my clothes dry slips to the floor. The squashed angry look on your face begins to melt away like the features of a wax mask in the sun. Your eyes rove a little.

God, I'd forgotten, you say. Or tried to forget. You step towards me and I step to meet you and the rough fabric of your shirt brushes my skin. My angles lose their acuteness immediately and begin to erode down like mountain peaks over the centuries, flattening out, creating fertile plains from barren valleys. Later, both wrapped in the blanket, I say, I really am sorry to hear about your mother, you know. Tell me what happened. You talk and I listen to your voice and I almost understand what the words mean. I think about my own mother and I think I will ring her tomorrow. We both talk then, all through the night, while the rain continues to piss down, battering on the tin roof, running down through cracks in the earth, soaking down, down towards the seeds hidden there, aching for wetness, for direction, for energy to head for the light.

Next morning, the rain has stopped. I lie curled in a happy ball in your bed and I hear you outside swearing as you try to start your bike to ride to work. I throw you my car keys out the window. You throw me the keys to your bike but of course I don't catch them. You knew I wouldn't.

I wander into the kitchen dreamily to make coffee. I have no classes today and I am filled with that sleek, creamy sense of well-being you get from not having anything you must do. Some of it could be attributed to the night, of course, the lovemaking, the holding. I feel languid and liquid smooth, like quicksilver, despite so little sleep. The coffee things are still out on the benchtop from last night. Normally you would have put them away before going to bed. You were always meticulous about things like that and I drove you mad. Lackadaisical, you used to say. I don't know where you found words like that. That one doesn't require much more than twice before it loses its meaning, if it had any in the first place. I fill the kettle, one of those ones with a spherical chrome surface that distorts your face like a mirror in a sideshow. My face in the kettle looks like I usually feel. There is no doubt I am distorted. I have had years to notice that I am not quite like other people in certain ways, that there is a kind of chaos in my head, but I've tried to cover it up, pass it off as eccentricity, something endearing. It didn't endear me to you. Not in the long run. It must've at first. You used to call me *Sugar*, as if we were in an old American movie or *A Streetcar Named Desire*. Now *he* was a bastard and she still loved him; why couldn't you have gone on loving me?

I spoon coffee into the plunger and imagine *you* doing it. I see your movements in my mind perfectly. I can rehearse them even after so long, all those movements of yours – bending to pick up my discarded, screwed-up pages, drying plates scrupulously, stretching skin between two fingers to shave cleanly, cupping your hand to push the hair off my forehead. What good does that kind of knowledge do anybody? Where does it go? What is it good for? I carry that useless information around in my brain, just taking up crucial space. I get it out occasionally in daydreams, in nightdreams, and some of these movement memories, some of my favourite ones, I take out to use when I'm alone in my bed. Even when I'm not alone. I know so many things about you better than I know about myself. The burden of the observer. In the end your observations of me were too much for you. Even though it was the motorbike dolly that brought things to a head. It was on its last legs before that. I always had a sneaking suspicion there was something I hadn't seen clearly enough. But then I feel like that most of the time. Like I'm on some time lapse mechanism and reality catches up with me later. Too late.

I pour boiling water from the gargoyle kettle onto the coffee. The air fills with delicious coffee-scented steam. I wonder what you're thinking now, at your computer, your coffee in a polystyrene cup beside you. I wonder is it the same for you, this strange dislocation in seeing each other again, knowing each other again instantly like you know a brother or sister, comfortably, deeply, but aware of the chasms – of experience, of secrets, of life, pain, love – that it would be impossible to bridge unless we were together for long enough to weave the last years into our awareness of each other. Surely, you can never catch up. Like Tristram Shandy forever trying to get ahead of his life. It must be impossible. And yet, when you meet someone new you think you will assimilate that person's history, that baggage, that particular thread, and weave it into the fabric of your life. The rich tapestry. Or the tatty rag.

I take my coffee back to bed. I've missed this bed, this room, this house. I've missed you. I have really missed you. It's been good for me in that it showed me I *did* care, I *could* care. I just couldn't care in a way that was comprehensible to you. Could I *now*? Is it worth trying to go against your nature to be something you aspire to being? Namely, loving in a way that other people see as loving, instead of in your own quirky style. I didn't used to think so. Now, I'm not so sure. Would it really have hurt me to try just that little bit harder, to meet you at least half way? Would it? The torment of hypotheticals. There is only one place to experiment and that's in the here and now. Thought experiments hold no water. How can a thought experiment get you anywhere? Those scientists with their on-again, off-again cat in a box. If their minds are such that they can imagine a here, not-here cat, they are in big trouble. They are probably in big trouble anyway considering they are looking for a big TOE. That's a joke. TOE. Theory of everything. I had a teacher in school who had a theory of everything. He was from Glasgow and he used to say, Everything is shite. It's up to you lot to make it better. Jesus, what a burden on our young shoulders. And have we? Have any of us done anything that has made a difference? I doubt it. Even our small personal successes have been ripples in a tidal pool on a beach, not even reaching the wide ocean. Small fish in a small pond, with not even enough sense to mate.

We had started to talk about children. Remember? I used to laugh and say, You want to hang out my dirty genes in public. Flippant as always. But underneath I was scared. I didn't admit it. What if I passed on my . . . affliction? I don't think you ever realised, that you ever put two and two together and got more than three. And I said I didn't like talking about my past so that cut off that line of inquiry. I knew at school, even before. I never quite understood what was going on, all the social stuff. Couldn't see the pitfalls, the traps, even the rewards. To me, things were simple, cut and dried. I couldn't play the game because I didn't know the rules. Everyone else had rules, inbuilt or learned. But something was missing in me. Some little deformed gene, some frayed piece of DNA had messed up my chances for having a best friend, for getting picked for the role of the Virgin Mary, for belonging. Only my parents knew, had known from the earliest signs, and they didn't let on. Not because they were ashamed or anything, just because they thought it might be better if I weren't singled out, given a label. They were right. As a child it was difficult but as I grew older I learned about me and people like me, and I developed a cover. I even developed. I watched other people's reactions, interactions. I learned about emotions. I knew what it was supposed to be like, but, in the same way a blind person can't imagine blue although he might have a deep intellectual understanding of it, I couldn't feel those things. Oh, I could feel pleasure, physiological impulses and releases. I was a good lover because I was never messed up with the emotional, just concentrated on the senses, pure and perfect. Love making was one of my favourite pastimes because then I was in my element and my carnality could be mistaken for fervour, even for love. It wasn't until I met you that I remotely felt that missing emotion of love, as if someone had just connected, albeit imperfectly, my heart to my body. I don't know how you did it. And you never knew you did. I try another thought experiment. Supposing I had told you. Hypothetical hell again. I didn't want you to think I was a freak, from next door to the distorting mirrors and the bearded lady. I didn't want you to be frightened off. Perhaps you wouldn't have been. Perhaps you would have been bigger than I gave you credit for. Perhaps you would have loved me just the same. Oh, Jesus, I'm getting as bad as the scientists.

Tabby, your cat, who is a tabby, of course, no irony in you at all, comes slinking around the door jamb into the bedroom. She mews in a wild way, starts purring so loudly I can hear her from the bed, then she breaks into a trot and leaps up on to me. We snuggle like the old friends we are. She stands on my chest and does the old quickstep, pawing and letting go of the blanket in fast time, purring like a motorbike running. Animals are easier. Animals and me get along just fine. I sometimes think that I am really some little animal, simple, totally sensuous, conscious in a black and white way, trapped inside the body of a human being. A mink? A sloth?

It dawns on me that it *is* the purring of a motorbike I can hear. I run to the window and there is a young man in blue overalls squatted by the motorbike. He is shaking his head. I pull on my clothes, which have dried overnight, and go out to him.

Hi, I say.

Hi, he says back without looking up. And continues, What's he doing leaving it out in the rain anyway?

He does a kind of a Tut, tut, with his mouth. I laugh.

Now he does look up. He stares at me as if I'm

demented. I straighten out the laughter until it is an ordinary voice again.

What are you doing?

He looks down to his work again, his hands fondling greasy parts lovingly. Pete sent me round to pump out the tank, see if there was any damage. Bloody vandals. I know what I'd do to 'em if ever I got my hands on 'em.

I imagine his greasy hands around my throat. Then I think how sweet you are not to let on, even to your mechanic, that it was me. Your Sugar. In a fit of jealousy.

Jealousy, I say out loud. I say it again. Jealousy.

The mechanic looks up again, suspiciously, then says, Yeah, probably, but there are plenty of other bikes you'd be more jealous of. A Harley. Or a Ducati. Dunno why they'd pick this one.

His voice goes on like the hum of traffic in the distance but my mind is on something else. It is on jealousy. That's what I felt last night. Again. I felt it when I caught them that time and I didn't recognise the choking, engulfing feeling for what it was. But I felt it. I *felt* it. I am jubilant.

I lean down and kiss the mechanic on the cheek. Bastards, I say, and laugh again as I skip into the house.

On hold

Francis, Tony and Xavier are about to arrive. I hear their voices when they are still some distance down the hospital corridor. Francis and Tony are arguing. They sound like a television left on in an upstairs flat, muffled but insistent. I can't make out what is under discussion – there's plenty to discuss – but I recognise the tone of Francis' voice from years of arguments. It would usually go something like this.

I don't want to pull rank here.

That's him. Francis.

Well, don't then.

That's me. Kim.

I'm the one with the PhD.

Him again. Taking turns from now on. We were always good at turn-taking. Lesson one in interpersonal relationships.

That's in palaeontology, darling. Not in relationships. In relationships we're equal.

Well, in fact, you've had a number of short relationships. And I've had one other relationship, which lasted fifteen years. So I think I'm in front there too.

You mean like a straight flush beats two pair?

What?

It's from gambling. Taking a risk.

I took a big risk taking you on.

This is usually where I begin to cry. I can't believe it's come to this. I had such high hopes.

Not the crying. Can't you do anything other than cry? Can't you take part in a reasonable, rational discussion?

Look, Francis. It upsets me. I cry. Cause and effect. I don't like it when you yell at me over such a little thing.

Little thing?

Francis is master of mountain from molehill. He's had practice. He has, after all, reconstructed entire skeletons out of two or three shards of bone.

I don't call humming under your breath a small thing. I was trying to think. I waited for five minutes. You must have noticed. I know you noticed. You did it just to annoy me.

Francis, I didn't notice. I hum. I don't notice. You've never been bothered by it before. Just tell me if it's bothering you. Don't build up a head of steam and let me have it.

It's not possible that you didn't notice.

I swear, Francis. Why get so riled up about it?

Because I was trying to think. And I couldn't. And it was your fault.

This is the point at which I leave the room. I know, I know. Not constructive. Nothing resolved. But yet again something was my fault. I could never guess ahead of time what it might be. I began to feel I was living on tenterhooks. I mean, we'd been living together for ten years all up, married for the last seven. My humming had never bothered him before. Another day it might be the way I left the shower curtain. Or cutting the bread crooked.

What was I doing, anyway, with someone who had a particular pair of socks for each day of the week? Who, everywhere in the world he went, sought out the same breakfast he had at home. I'd say to relax, drink the local caffeine brew, eat the local pastries or fish soup or whatever. Everything was always difficult. Someone was always upsetting him. And if someone else wasn't, there was always me.

Palaeontology has a lot to answer for. In palaeontology untidy loose ends aren't allowed. It's a science of tidying up loose ends. Everything has to be made to fit perfectly. I had come to understand that I was a loose end.

I always imagined it was called palaeontology for the pale people who studied it. All alone in their labs.

Then out into the bright sunshine directing people like me, willing to sweat it, and turning pink before our eyes. That's how we met. On a dig. I thought it would be exciting. At the coalface, so to speak. It turned out that that idea was more literal than metaphorical. Up a cliff, on a ledge two feet wide, tapping away at rock for hours with a tiny hammer, passing anything that might be something down the line. And never with much of a clue what it was all about. Not the big picture.

That's how Francis won me over. He supplied the big picture one night in a two-horse town on the edge of the Negev desert in Israel, over numerous glasses of aniseed-flavoured arak. That was my drink – he drank imported Australian wine.

It's like this, he said. What we need is a complete jaw bone. If we get a jaw bone, we can prove this fish had begun to change the shape of its mouth to accommodate a different type of feeding, or rather, a new supply of food.

Perhaps it was about then I decided to move into the area of people. After all, we were having a conversation about a fish which lived three hundred and sixty-three million years ago. I had only been dallying with palaeontology as a possible direction in which to take anatomy. I had thought that out in the desert I would learn something about the nature of mankind. Instead, fish jaws. Gills. Francis was still talking, unaware of the career change happening across the table. He did seem to be a bit boring, a bit full of himself. Didn't he know it was polite to ask a question or two about the person you're with? I couldn't work out if this was supposed to be a come-on or not. If it was, surely he would have reached over and taken my hand on the table. I had left both hands there, in plain view, the entire time.

When he asked me back to his room for a nightcap, I thought that was probably all it would be. I was in no hurry to get back to my own shared quarters in a kibbutz dorm called a *skubiot*, otherwise known by us as 'the hovel'. But then, well, it was nothing short of sweeping me off my feet. He played a song on the guitar; my heart melted. Even women in science fall in love for the silliest reasons. At the start of the next term, we moved in together. That is, I moved into his spacious and pristine house. It was a given that my flat, which he called 'bohemian', was out of the question.

Did I mention that he was twenty years older than me? Not that it made any difference. But I was a bit embarrassed by the cliché. Professor and student. A year later they made it illegal for such a thing to happen on campus. But I changed courses and people didn't always make the connection between the two of us. It didn't matter: I was happy. Happy as Larry, whoever

Larry was. I was in love. This man was a genius. He was doing ground-breaking work on the Devonian period, which might well change the current understanding of why our ancient ancestors had abandoned their home in water and opted to live on land.

We wanted to be a modern couple – equal, respectful. And that would have been easy if it hadn't been for my many faults. I don't know how it was he didn't pick them up in the first place. With an eye accustomed to spotting the most minute change in structure of a bone, you'd think he'd have noticed that I was opinionated, a bit sloppy around the house, that I liked to drink and to laugh out loud a lot. Strangely enough, he didn't notice until we were married.

Adaptation, Francis, I would say. That's how we made it as a species.

Perhaps you could do some adapting to my needs, he would reply.

I read somewhere that marriage still makes men think they are boss. It's as if a green light goes off in the ancient part of their brain and, despite claims to feminism, respect for women in general, and love for their wives in particular, they begin to give orders, impose restrictions and express concern when wives don't comply.

We would go out to dinner with friends – his – and I would put forward an opinion different to the one he had expounded. Across the table I would see my mistake. I would be in for it when we got home. We would argue through the night and then I would get up at seven to go and teach a class of first year medical students. As it went on, I simply got worn out.

Coming home got harder. The thought of coming in the front door and finding out what I had done wrong that day made me tired. I took to stopping at a café. Or a park. Or a beach. Just a break between work and home, I would tell myself. To gather my thoughts. Gird my loins, more like.

And then I discovered another place for my breather – the potting shed. I hadn't been inside before. I suppose all that digging in earth and chipping at stone I'd done every summer holiday meant I wasn't keen to take up gardening as a hobby. And I never saw Francis get his hands dirty once. We employed a gardener, Tony, who came in once a fortnight to keep things in order. I'd seen him from the upstairs window taking instruction from Francis.

Nothing taller than me, Francis instructed, holding his hand flat above his head as if to determine which of the men was taller. Tony looked puzzled.

You mean you don't want any of the trees taller than you? You want me to cut the tops out when they get to here. He held his hand flat at nose level.

That's right, Francis said. I don't want things getting out of hand.

Righty-ho, said Tony with a smile. It was a big smile too, I noticed. Bigger than I was used to.

I was usually away at work when Tony came to do the garden on a Wednesday. Occasionally I'd pass him on the way out as I came in and we'd stop and exchange a few words. Nothing special, but always pleasant. So it was a surprise when, on one of my recovery stops at the potting shed, I opened the door to see the outline of a man against the window. The sudden dark after the sunlight outside meant that's all it was at first, an outline.

The outline moved. There was a gleam of white. As my eyes adjusted to the dark I could see that the white was Tony's smile.

Sorry, I said. And then wondered why I said it. It was my potting shed. Ours. But I'd become accustomed to apologising for almost everything I did.

No, *I'm* sorry. Changed my day because something came up. I didn't mean to startle anyone.

Right. I was just . . .

And then, god knows why, I burst into tears. Looking back, I think it was because of the way he said, No, *I'm* sorry. Something wasn't my fault! Hallelujah!

I'm sure Tony meant it to be a comforting hug, nothing more. But it was so very comforting, and I was so desperately in need of comfort, that I couldn't let go. I cried and cried and somehow or other he began kissing the tears away. Then kissing my mouth. Then we were taking off each other's clothes. In the back of my mind, was a little voice asking if my whole life was to be made up of clichés, but soon I wasn't thinking of anything other than the hum of my body.

What! I shrieked. Tony and I were sharing a cigarette after the sex. Once you've embarked on a cliché, you might as well do it properly.

What's wrong with that? he asked, reasonably enough.

I promised myself that if I ever had anything to do with another man I wouldn't touch one who had a PhD.

Well, that gives us a year, he said. I won't be finished until the middle of next year.

I thought you were a gardener! I pouted. I wanted my cliché back.

Only on Wednesdays. This week, Thursday. You can't live on a PhD scholarship, you know. Not what I'd call live anyway.

And he did know how to live, my Tony. That's what I called him privately. Well, it was all private. He was my secret. My secret lover. It remained a cliché after all. Wife, many years younger than husband, has affair with younger man, gardener. But he wasn't a gardener. He was completing his PhD in bio-chemistry. Bio-chemistry is what happened between us. That's what I'd say, looking back on it. And he made me feel sane and strong instead of undermined. I spent more and more time with him and, somewhere inside me, I was happy again.

How did you get into medicine? Tony finally asked me one day. People always get around to it. Usually they aren't ready for long answers. They expect, My father was a doctor, so . . . I tell him about my childhood, how I was fascinated from the beginning with the body. How I drove my mother mad asking about each of my teeth as they came through the gum. The eye tooth. The molar. Which will last how long? And then, Mummy? Permanent teeth? Forever? They will last forever? Wisdom teeth! Now they sounded truly fascinating.

From the time I was five I collected teeth. I told friends in prep class that I offered more than the tooth fairy. In my bedroom I kept the teeth in old egg cartons and shoe boxes with cardboard sections glued into them. I was amazed by these pieces of people, which simply fell out and were replaced. It was harder to get hold of adult teeth, but every once in a while I'd hear of someone having a tooth out and ask them if they wouldn't mind keeping it for me. Everyone thought I would grow up to be a dentist.

But it wasn't about dentistry. It was the way these teeth captured so much about the whole person. I learned from television documentaries and encyclopedias that specialists could tell such things as age, diet and illnesses of a dead person from their teeth. I wanted to be the one who examined the teeth of a Bronze Age man and discovered that he used his teeth to hold the spears he bound. Naturally, I did Life Sciences and headed towards palaeontology. Then I met a pale man and instead ended up in medicine. Embryology to be exact.

I'm interested in bodies too, you know, said Tony. Particularly yours.

Embryology is how I came to be on television. If you've ever seen a documentary on the human body, which, with wonderful new camera devices, traces the path of sperm through a vagina into the womb to rally around an egg, then that vagina was probably mine. It was an obvious decision. I was a scientist. And I was pregnant. They needed a willing pregnant woman. I thought I might as well do something worthwhile for humanity since I was already pregnant. At the time I didn't think the pregnancy itself all that worthwhile. After all, every living creature replicates, reproduces. Nothing special about that. But this way, I could do my bit for mankind by being host to cameras and electrodes, X-rays and the like. By having the whole of my pregnancy and birth mapped electronically and images generated ad infinitum. I got so caught up in the process I almost forgot that at the end of it all I would have a real live baby. When I got home from hospital, there weren't even any clothes ready for it. For him. For Xavier.

Darling Xavier. He sits to my right, holding my right hand in both of his small ones. Although shortly he will go off to a friend's for the afternoon. He has just told me so. To my left sits Tony, holding my left hand in his left hand, and tenderly stroking my inner forearm with his right. At the end of the bed sits Francis, ramrod straight. Stonily. Fitting for a palaeontologist. Inside, I laugh. I wish I could tell someone this thought. Tell Tony. I would like to grin, to tell them how much I'm enjoying this.

For years I tried to persuade Francis to hold my hand. He considered handholding unseemly. Adolescent. I asked him if he'd held hands with girls when he was an adolescent and he hemmed and hawed and couldn't recall. I knew he had not. Francis was a man who couldn't hold hands. Unless, that is, they were the newly developed hands of creatures millions of years old. Those hands he would hold till the cows came home.

Francis doesn't believe I can hear. He punctuates any argument about the matter with the phrase 'vegetative state'. I would like to punch him. Tony says he's read the literature and knows it's possible. Francis says that particular writer is a maverick, not a scientist at all. A witch doctor. Tony says the man's been proven right in the past. That people have responded and come out of comas not only months but years long. Francis says he doesn't believe anything he hasn't seen with his own eyes. Like the split atom, Tony quips to Francis. To me he says, You act on hunches, don't you, darling. Intuition.

Francis winces at the endearment, I'm sure. But Tony's right. Motherhood helped me there. Prior to Xavier I could lecture on the reproductive system and lift out the ovaries of cadavers, name and analyse. After Xavier I was thrown into some other kind of atavistic knowing, understanding his cries instantly from their tone, determining needs from tiny gestures, feeling in the pit of my stomach my son's need of me. Layers were peeled away. I was peeled back to the girl collecting teeth without much understanding of why, compelled by a lifeline laid down in my genes.

Later, after Xavier has gone, I hear Tony saying to Francis. Look, it's a bit like that French philosopher. The one who said even if you don't believe in God it's worth going through the motions just in case it turns out there's something in it after all. The wager. A bob each way. I don't hear an answer. In my mind's eye, I see Francis roll his eyes.

Tony has asked Francis to bring in photographs from home. He holds them up in front of my face and talks about them. He seems to know I want the communion photo. What was I – eight? The white dress and veil. Child bride of God. I often think of myself as the little girl in the photo in her first communion dress. Hands held fervently together. Squarely, trustingly. I can't say now whether I believed in God or not, but I certainly went through the motions. It was the motions I liked. All that ritual. Blessings. Sacrifice. Forgiveness.

Once, in the middle of one of our arguments, I went to this same photo album and took out a photograph of me as a child of two or three. Dressed in a funny kind of one-piece sunsuit beside a paddling pool. Hands nonchalantly pushed into a pocket in the terry-towelling. A lick of hair curled up like a cockatoo's crest on top of my head. I held the photo out. Francis was almost apoplectic because I had walked from the room while he was speaking. Yes, I know, respect and being heard and all that. But he had been going on in the same vein for more than an hour.

Look, I said. Look, this is me.

He was bewildered. Completely bewildered. I pushed the photo forward, forced him to take it into his hands and look at it.

I still feel like that little girl inside, I said.

Don't be so ridiculous and sentimental.

I am that little girl. I am. That's me. Still finding my way. Not perfect, but okay. And all you want to do is harangue her with your interminable arguments and explanations as to why you are, again, right. You're going to take her shine away.

To his credit he was actually looking at the photograph now.

You weren't that cute, he finally said.

Before I could react, he looked at me and smiled that old smile. Which was all it took. But it had to come from him. There was nothing on this earth I could do that would end it. Even when I apologised, he would not forgive me. It was the unsmiling face for days on end that I found hardest.

If one of them were to ask me what I believe in, I would say the will to live. In this, as in so much else, the individual is like the species. I believed it before, but since the accident, since I've been in this state, I *know* it to be true.

They're having a DNA test done. They don't mention it. It would be unseemly. Xavier, bless his soul, remains happily unaware. Or does he? They've always had an affinity, the oddball Xavier and my gardener/lover, Tony. Unbeknownst to Francis, Tony would sometimes pick Xavier up from school for me. If I had a particularly vexing experiment. Or, yes, I should admit it now, if I just wanted to see these two together, just see them, and try to tell. You'd think you would always be able to tell. Outsiders might do better, given all the facts. After all, if they could only see my toes and Xavier's there'd be no doubt in their minds that I was his mother. Hammer toes. People were once advised to have an operation. I was advised by a school nurse. My parents, happily, ignored. I followed suit, despite my calling, with regard to Xavier. Xavier ended up doing the same tricks as me, squashing the middle toe over the second toe like they were mating. They were never going to be a flat row of toes.

His ears. Now his ears were a puzzle. Not like mine, not like Francis', not like Tony's. But odd, definitely odd. Some kind of throwback. Francis and I both know a lot about throwbacks, and that's what we'd always tell each other. Ears that stuck out to the side. Cute when young, but not so cute later on, I worried. Nevertheless, I found those ears the most lovable feature of my altogether lovable son. If anyone had suggested what this feeling for my son would be like before he was born, I would have pooh-poohed them. I was a scientist. I knew the process. I was happy for the whole world to watch the process taking place inside me because I knew that this was the most ordinary process in the world. Procreation. Continuation. It's what life forms strive for. The next generation. It's what evolution is all about.

It isn't something special. That, anyway, was the kind of statement I made during my pregnancy and labour, when I was a kind of celebrity, me and baby Xavier, both watched by millions in what I call our contortionist months. But afterwards, well, that was different.

I couldn't believe it at first, when I discovered I was pregnant. I was a specialist in all this. A mistake couldn't happen to me. I did two home pregnancy tests in one of the staff bathrooms at the hospital and, although I know they never lie, I kept looking at the second one expecting it to change its mind. As the news dawned on me, I thought, yes, it was obvious. An embryologist really should have a baby, really should experience the growth of an embryo in her own body. Francis and I had decided not to have children. There were more than enough children in the world. It was a self-indulgent act, having a child. Did we want to bring a child into this world where want or desperation were the staple for most? Oh yes, we had all the arguments lined up like a row of soldiers. We were both busy scientists, making a contribution to the world. Having a baby was something anyone could do. Francis had suggested there was a deep irony in the fact that nobodies had children and that contributing professionals like us, with the right genes, chose not to. His spin on this made me squirm. All babies got the same beginning, except for genes of course, but essentially the same. They developed in a predictable way. Birth was the same for all women, regardless of their position in the world. Or was it? No, I knew social status already had an effect on the foetus healthwise, and on its chances of survival. Born equal? Not exactly. Biology is everything, Francis repeated like a stuck record.

There is another voice in the room now. I recognise it. It's the orderly who sometimes helps to lift me when the bed is changed.

Which of you is Dr Francis Leicester?

I am, says Francis in a tight voice.

He is, says Tony. No other doctors in the room. Can't you tell?

Somehow Tony always manages to put laughter into his voice. The situation may be tense but Tony is one of those people who accepts the ups and downs of life. He doesn't expect perfection. He never did finish his PhD. Something interesting came up during his experiments and he got side-tracked into investigating it in depth. Sometimes the accidental things turn out to be more important, he said at the time. I don't care about the PhD. I can always come back to it. Besides, he joked, as you don't want a lover with a PhD, this way we can continue being lovers.

A very big loose end is what Francis would think.

I hear the rip of an envelope. Inside my prone body

the presence of these two men becomes so large and so heated I want to scream. I'm sure I will burst. Tony. Of course it will be Tony. A baby would be just too much of a loose end for Francis. He would never allow his body to betray him by making a baby. That's what I often told myself anyway. But life worked well the way it was. Francis was a good steady provider and a good father. Tony was a butterfly. I had no desire to pin him down.

I hear the shuffling of papers, an intake of breath.

Well? says Tony.

Another rustling of paper across my bed.

Jesus, says Tony.

I don't think Jesus had anything to do with it, says Francis.

So I was right, it's Tony. Somehow I am shocked, nevertheless. Another part of me always assumed Francis was the father, since that was his role.

It's okay, says Francis.

What? It's okay? I can't believe Francis is saying this.

I knew all along, he continues.

You knew? I think. You knew? I want to scream.

You knew? says Tony in a cracking voice.

I had a vasectomy well before Kim and I got together. I just never told her. I always meant to.

You what!

My god! says Tony.

Tony always calls himself an atheist. Funny how at moments of stress he can only intone the names of the Christian heroes.

But the test? says Tony.

Yes, why the bloody test? I want to yell.

Just in case. Sometimes these things aren't a hundred per cent.

You brought up someone else's child! You knew Xavier wasn't yours!

Tony sounds flabbergasted. And, if I weren't already, I would be speechless.

I knew I could give him a good life. I am giving him a good life.

Over the next few hours the two men discuss what they will do. I have never heard Francis sound even somewhat humble, till now. Tony sounds nervous and excited all at the same time. They decide they will leave things as they are except that Tony will spend more time with Xavier.

Xavier will have two fathers, Tony jokes. One nature and one nurture.

Dad! Xavier bursts into the room and I hear Francis grunt as he receives a big Xavier hug.

Tony! Xavier runs around the bed and hugs Tony. He squeals at something, probably Tony tickling him.

Then my son comes to the bedside and takes my hand. He doesn't seem to have noticed anything strange about the atmosphere.

Hello, Mum, he says in his beautiful piping voice. How was your afternoon? Same old, same old?

An image of my boy's face floats within me. Sparkling eyes, mop of light brown hair, and those ears. All at once, I know where I have seen those ears before. Up close. That intern from Canada. I remember joking to one of the nurses that his ears were like the prawn crackers served by the local Chinese restaurant. She'd said, Yes, makes you want to bite them, hey. Which is what I'd done some weeks later in one of the store rooms. How could I have missed it? I've hidden the truth from myself for such a long time. That quick scramble in the store comes back to me in minute lucid detail as if I am re-experiencing it. His hands on my breasts, my hips. His thighs so unexpectedly brown. Next comes the pregnancy, my belly ballooning out for the cameras and television crew. Now the birth, lit so brightly that I am in that birthing room all over again. Inside myself I'm screaming with the pain and loving it all at the same time. Images are falling thick and fast and in full colour. Everything is speeding up and I feel as if I am drawing closer and closer to some end point. It's hard to keep track of what is being said in the room. Goodbyes, it sounds like. Wait!

I want to scream. A brush of lips on my hand. Tony's? Xavier's? Three muffled sets of footsteps leave together and no one is there to hear the first sound I have made in four months.

Pram rage

From where I hide under the bed all I see are two legs, or possibly three, through the bottom of the floor-to-ceiling window. Frosted glass diminishes them to fuzzy sticks. I think of a circus man-on-stilts and how he'd be able to see over the rooftop into the backyard, see the line of white cloths snapping in the salt breeze, fourteen flags of surrender. I look across to where Liam lies in his rocker making alert bird movements with his head, looking at wall, window, me, floor, with equal wide-eyed interest. I hold my index finger to my lips. He opens his mouth in a round gummy smile, kicks his feet up, puts both fists in the air in a secret salute of collusion.

Footsteps falter at the corner of the house. Will the legs go round the corner, peek into my backyard? It would be overstepping familiarity, even curiosity, whoever owns the legs. I don't know anyone here well enough for them to saunter into the yard. But if they think there is no one home?

A shuffle, a scrape. Then steps crunch up the giveaway gravel of the drive and meet bitumen's sudden silence. I breathe a long breath out.

I lie under the bed for another five minutes, counting sixteen slats in the base, and pulling faces at Liam to keep him silently laughing. When I clamber out, his face collapses into a purple wrinkled plum and I hear a wail approaching from far away like the high-pitched whistle of a train down a tunnel. Before it arrives, I have his mouth near enough to my left nipple to clamp on like a limpet and we both calm down in the sure knowledge of what the next ten minutes of our lives hold in store. In the morning he sucks like a calf. With steady gusto. If you've ever put your finger in a calf's mouth you'll know. Stories used to go around about boys who put their willy in calves' mouths. I guess they knew what they were doing. I remember a man who had to get a plumber because he had his radish stuck up the bath tap. I suppose he knew what he was doing, too. It seems that if you have one you'll try it in likely places.

Strong, rhythmic sucking. I fall into a state of bliss looking down at his gloating face. Neck, I think. I drag my gaze away, look straight ahead, eyes on a point just below horizontal. Neck muscles have become steel hawsers, rigid enough to rig a bridge. Shoulder muscles hard as rocks. Joints creak like my ironing board. Why spend so long doing antenatal pelvic floor exercises, swaying hips, limbering thighs? We should have lifted weights, flexed spines. My joints need oiling, as if Liam is sucking out every drop of moisture into his supple perfect body. These bones are too old.

Ridgety didge, we three on a bridge, and who do you think will jump?

The sucking eases. There are small snores. I wait, and half-hearted sucks start up again, barely there like dream sucking he does in his sleep. I wait again. He falls away. I put him down to sleep.

In my big bed, Liam is tiny, this creature who looms so large, huge, in my day. His hands are thrown up beside his head in abandon. I tiptoe from the room and run to my computer.

It's a novel I want, that I have, somewhere inside me. I feel it the way I could feel Liam in utero with a sure knowledge that only lacked external appearance. But it needs a wide valley of time to flow down. The small gullies, declivities, I offer are scraps. Instead, clotted lines gather in my mouth like posset. Language has turned to milk, separating into watery whey of baby talk and heavy curds of poetry. Nothing is left. But I don't want poetry. I don't *want* it. I must have my novel, something big and cumbersome and flawed, gestating slowly and going off in unexpected directions.

I remember I haven't turned the washing machine on and rush to do it. I stand listening to its comforting motor thrum, counting beats, pulsing, rocking from side to side with its music. Where is Brian now, I wonder. Brisbane? Sydney still? Touring. Seeing the sights. I know what sights he'll be seeing.

I am still standing there when the washing machine judders to a stop at the end of its cycle. I unload it. Then I remember I didn't add fabric softener to the wash, so I pitch everything back in and turn it on again. I go outside to bring in yesterday's dry nappies. I hold them to my nose and feel I'm in an advertisement, authenticity offered up on the domestic altar of television. There's no TV here.

Liam's blue and white quilt isn't quite dry so I spread it over the paling fence in a patch of weak sun. In America, runaway slaves knew that a blue and white quilt hung on a fence meant they were welcome. It was a safe house.

I fill today's nappy buckets trying not to breathe in bleach fumes. I gather up nappies already dirty and rinse them off. I put them in buckets. I put the kettle on. I am coping.

Polly put the kettle on. Suky got the whisky out. We'll all go free.

A friend told me how she once found herself watching

nappies go round and round in her washing machine, and weeping. It was twenty years before she told anyone.

Liam cries, but he's dreaming. What dreams can he already have that demand cries?

I must go to town soon. I can't keep avoiding it. Perhaps today. Perhaps this afternoon. If Liam has a good sleep. If I go later there won't be so many people. And it's not a big town, not a real city. I saw a newspaper article about a man in the city charged with assaulting a woman who was moving too slowly with her pram. It wasn't an isolated incident. They're calling it pram rage. Even the pram rage man was a baby once.

I creep in to peek at him. He lies still, his face perfectly composed, as if chiselled from marble, delicately carved lips and brow as harmonious as a sonata. I can't get enough of looking at him.

When Liam was still in the womb it was like being blind, like knowing someone intimately but not what they look like. When people blind from birth are given sight, faces of friends and family are extraordinary to them. *So beautiful and each one different*.

Sometimes they close their eyes, go back to their known world, their *before*.

I notice on the palms of Liam's hands, spread like small stars on the sheet, that there are black lines where lint has gathered in his life lines.

I turn the kettle on again, empty the washing machine. As I peg the bright white squares – twelve of them – in a neat row I see, through a gap in bushes at the side of the house, one of my neighbours walking his dog, heading for the beach. I duck down behind the fence holding a wet nappy against my chest. A bee buzzes around my head then lands on the sweet cloth in my fist. It's a big fuzzy black and yellow storybook bee. I try to count its stripes as it hovers but it moves off each time I come close to getting it right.

Buzzy buzzy bee, what can you see? Fuzzy fuzzy bee, would you like to be me?

I peg the last nappies out and go inside to make coffee. I turn on the radio. It is a talkback show about birth. A baby is born every eight seconds, someone says. I count. One, two, three, four, five, six, seven, eight. And I think of the ones that aren't born, all those discarded foetuses. The unborn. In Milano, that best-dressed Italian city, they've begun putting signs on rubbish skips asking people – women – to think again before throwing away their baby. When Liam was born, an Aboriginal friend told me her people would call him a rubbish baby, on account of him being so small. For her it's an endearment.

When I open the fridge to get milk, there is none. There are two eggs and three apples. Yes, I will have to go to town today.

Egg and apple omelette, egg and apple pie. Grease the tin, throw it in, and bake it all on high.

The morning is almost over. Mornings are best. I love waking to Liam the lion cub, a smooth bundle of brown energy in the bed beside me. He growls and kicks and scratches. He squeals with delight when I tickle him. I take his nappy off and he is a totally free new being. His grin is mad. His hands pluck delight out of thin air. His own toes in front of his face amaze. He plays till his cries change key and I know he is hungry. I pull him in to my breast and we curl and suckle. All through the night we have fed like this in a quiet dance, turning over and over each other. It is slowing now as he feeds less often and somehow I miss the hectic blurred whirling of the first weeks.

Next comes our bath. We play more than wash and his limbs are a frog's, born to water. I lift him above my head and he shrieks with laughter, my water bird, arms spread, feathers dripping. He basks on the island of my chest, lifting his head with an ancient strength. My salamander. He is every young creature. Dreams of kittens drowned and rabbits shot come to haunt me.

After this morning's bath I wipe a flat wet surface into the steamy mirror and look at my body. Not bad considering. Beneath the curve of belly is a straight plum-coloured line, a splodge of lurid purple above and below on one side, from infection, like a determinedly set mouth with garish drunkenly-applied lipstick. I am a loose woman. My body is loose. Breasts are functional but not erotic. I feel them lengthening. Soon they will be the breasts of women I see on television in famine-struck countries. Dugs. Babies don't stir from mother's hip. They reach and grab and stick the empty thing in their mouth. So much for the eroticism, the sensuality of breastfeeding. Only occasionally, when his mouth moves lightly to the end of the nipple, does his sucking echo teasingly in my clitoris. It is like a name I almost remember.

My husband is having an affair with the second fiddle. She is playing second fiddle and so am I. I have been. Not any more. He won't even know where to look for me.

In town I try to push the stroller nonchalantly, assured. I see in a shop window that I look as if I'm mowing a lawn. I straighten my back, relax my shoulders, slow down, breathe. I see another mother with a pusher coming my way and get a smile ready for the usual exchange. I wonder for a moment what her life is like. She walks straight past me without even looking. Her baby is screaming.

Two elderly women stop ahead of me and incline their heads towards the stroller. Can I merely slow down for them to peep and murmur? Now they have stepped right into my path and I will have to stop altogether. They lean in and coo. Liam coos back and I think how it must look to him, two faces in clouds of grey looming in front of him blocking the light. I smile and nod and push forward. They scuttle backwards out of the way, almost toppling over. I take a deep breath. Only one more block before the fruit and vegetable shop.

To market, to market to buy a new life. Home again, home again, nobody's wife.

Ahead is a café with tables outside and I momentarily consider sitting there. How would it feel to sit leisurely sipping coffee, watching the world go by, flipping through a magazine? I don't slow down. At the last table a woman sits alone. She gathers herself up and leans out, eyes on the stroller. I sigh inwardly and determine not to slow my pace. I take a wider path around her chair but she leans right out and peers in. I don't slow but I hear her words as she leans back into her chair. *That baby's almost dead.* Now I do stop. I turn to where she sits with her back to me, a youngish woman with dark hair to her shoulders. I stare at her back but she doesn't turn. I start to shake. I want to run. I put my left foot down carefully, then my right, and walk away slowly, head up, my hands gripping the pusher handle to quell the shaking. I stop and look back again but this time the chair is empty. I walk right round the block and don't stop at the fruit shop. I put Liam in the car and drive home, ring an order through to the local shop and ask for groceries to be delivered to my front doorstep.

Liam has fallen asleep in the car capsule by the time we lurch into the garage. I run inside and turn the shower on full blast. When I start to undress I realise I have worn my T-shirt inside out all day. I stand under streaming, scalding water and cry for so long I think I will disappear down the plughole.

I sit at my computer and watch the screen saver. Fish drift from left to right, right to left. I count them but after a while can't tell if I am counting the same fish or not. I start over again. Liam wakes before I touch the keyboard.

The next morning a load of washing drowns out the crunch of gravel and there is a knock at the door before I can get to the bedroom to hide. I stand in the kitchen prevaricating. Liam is already asleep after a restless night of feeding so frequently he seemed to be one of the oysters out on the island, clamped to rock. The harder you pull the harder they hang on. I walk there over rippled sand, past the jetty where children fish, whenever the tide is out, Liam a kangaroo joey in his cloth pouch. I pick up loose oysters and when I've opened them back at the house, gouging fingers with the screwdriver, throw them on the gas barbecue I found in the shed. I've given up on the ones clinging to rocks. If they're that attached to life, let them be.

There is another knock. I will have to answer. Whoever it is must know someone is in. They'll have heard the washing machine. They'll have seen the car. I run to the bathroom and drag a comb through my hair. It looks the same.

I open the door and say nothing. The man standing there says nothing either. I have the distinct feeling he is smelling me, taking in my scent, and am suddenly conscious of my own odours. Sicked-up milk and unwashed skin. He is an almost-old man. He has grey hair and a walking stick. His face is brown and neatly pleated as if he's been to the dry-cleaners. He is what people call dapper. Dressed to the nines even at this time of morning. Whatever this time of morning is. I notice a small silver pin in one lapel – a pair of binoculars.

I heard you're a writer, he says.

I was, I say. Now I'm a mother.

I wondered if you needed any help.

Help?

Yes, you know, being here on your own with the baby and all.

Jesus. Small towns. I say, I don't need any help.

Are you sure?

Quite sure.

Then, I'd love to visit and talk books sometimes. Not many people hereabouts read books.

What do they read, then?

Oh, the local newspaper. Births. Deaths.

I snort like a horse and the man lifts his head at the sound, puzzled. I suddenly realise he is blind. I thought they were simply rheumy old eyes but they are sightless.

Rich man, blind man, beggar man, thief. All of them, each one, will take him a wife.

Are you blind?

Ah. You've noticed. A bit slow, I'd say.

I am a bit slow these days. I didn't mean to be rude, I say. I look at the binocular pin. The man is a master of irony.

I'm used to it now. It's been three years. And they were on their way out for some time before that. A kind of fade-out like the end of some movies. I just wish I'd seen the orange-bellied parrot before my peepers went completely.

You're a bird watcher?

I was. Now I'm a blind man.

Touché.

Seriously though. I've always read a lot. Now I get hear-a-book. I can't read my beloved books. I can't see my beloved birds. But I would love to talk about books.

I'm not feeling all that sociable at the moment. This is the longest conversation I've had in weeks.

I gathered that.

Oh yes?

The whole place knows you're here and don't go out. Where did you think you were? New York? I'm not asking any questions. Just offering. I know it can be hard with a little one on your own. There was a woman hereabouts – you might have heard – who put her baby girl in the back of the car and drove off the jetty at high tide in the middle of the night.

Jesus.

Yes. So. What if I come tomorrow for coffee? I'll bring some cake.

I don't even know you.

I'm the good Samaritan.

With that he doffs his doffable hat, the kind you hardly ever see these days, taps his cane about in front and to the side and turns to walk the path to the drive. I'm Hans, he calls out without turning to look at me. Why would he?

The next morning I hurry through our routine. I get out the coffee plunger and grind coffee. I set out mugs and plates. I pace. I sit at the computer. I go in to check on Liam. He looks as serene as a boy monk asleep on a stone pillow after a long morning of devotion.

When I hear footsteps on gravel, I jump although I'm

expecting them. I open the door while he is feeling for the right place to knock.

Hello, Hans.

Hello, Deirdre.

You know my name.

Of course. Your mail is delivered to the post office.

I see.

I don't.

I realise after a pause that he is being funny and I laugh foolishly, endlessly, still holding the door open, Hans still standing there.

Come in. I've put things out for coffee.

Listen, says Hans. I haven't come to give you more work. I do know it can be hard. I just wanted you to have some company.

Even if I didn't want any.

Even if you didn't want any. It's not good to be alone all the time.

I'm not alone. There's Liam.

We are sitting with our cups of coffee on the small verandah at the back of the house, when I hear Liam's cry. I bring him out into the sunshine and this time I see Hans' nose lift and quick intakes of air.

Ah, he says. What a sweet smell – the smell of baby sleep. And he reaches his hand out until he feels fragile skull, downy hair.

I put Liam into his rocker on the verandah boards with a swinging mirror above him. He gazes, waves his fists about.

Do you have children? I ask then bite down on my own question. What presumption. What a tin of worms. I know it as it leaves my mouth.

Yes. Two boys. Grown up now. Gone.

They grow?

Yes. Quickly.

I try to imagine time being more assertive than in recent days. I rarely look at a clock. I can't imagine months, years.

And I had a daughter.

Had?

Yes. The story I told you yesterday. About the woman who drove off the jetty. She was my wife.

I'm glad he can't see my face. My mouth is a black cave. A scream reverberates silently in the opened space. There is no air. I find myself with my head in my hands, sobbing like there is no bottom to it.

I know, he is saying. I know. I just wish I had known then.

He comes regularly from then on and we sit on the back verandah drinking coffee, Liam offering salutes and smiles and watching the wind. I read to Hans. Anything from contemporary writers to classics. He laps it up. Liam gurgles delightedly when I pause. Hans' dead eyes close and he will sit not moving a muscle until I stop. Sometimes I read what I have been writing – the poetry. He has little to say about it except it is good that I write it. The other stuff I read, the novels, we talk about for longer than it takes to read them. He knows a lot. He has read a lot. I would say he is wise.

One day he suggests a walk out to the island so I bundle Liam, marsupial-like, into the carry-pouch and we set off.

I want to show off, Hans says as we walk on to the beach. I want you to see how much I see, even without seeing.

He tells me where we have come out of the dunes onto the beach below the jetty, tells me where the island lies, what the sky looks like, what plants are nearby. Memory, he says, is our greatest gift. And our curse.

For once I don't try to count sand ripples as I walk. Two birds wing past and land on the beach in front of us.

Oyster catchers, Hans says. See their orange beaks.

I would have been amazed in the past but I am beyond amazement. I accept everything. You know from the sound of their wings? I ask.

And the way they land, he says. And I cheated. I heard

their calls as they flew in. You find ways.

Liam squirms in the pouch, trying to look to the side, behind, his blue eyes wide. He is snuggled in against my chest and for once doesn't want to be there. He strains outwards to the world. He roars with the frustration of it and the oyster catchers take to air only to land again within a few yards. The tide is low and sand stretches away to the island with only a narrow channel left like a moat before it. The rippled sand is pocked by tops of crab holes, a chaotic braille under our bare feet. We stop and stand in the middle of sand flats with heads lifting, turning, each absorbing in our own way wind, salt air, water, sand, sun, bird cries, island, sky.

Adult education

Going home was the worst. Being part of that slow drain from the city, as if someone somewhere had pulled a plug. Sucked down wide streets to underground stations, onto buses taking them west, down to the quay and onto ferries heading inland along the river, or to the north shore for more buses, or to find cars, if they were lucky, that were left in the morning. All focused on the end point. The home. Perhaps a stop along the way for a coffee and the paper or a quick dive into a pub. It could look as if everyone was escaping something, as if some disaster had happened in the city centre – not an outrage like New York, everyone would be running then – but something long-expected, drilled for, inevitable.

For her it was the beginning of the end. For nine hours she was part of the pulse of things – chatter and banter, work, timetables, phone calls, bright office lights. Laughter over coffee. Not that she was in the middle of all that. But she felt included, as if she was inside the bright bubble, not outside looking in. Now, as she watched out the window for glimpses of the harbour, she felt the bubble fading. Within minutes she was at Bondi Junction station. Only a few minutes' wait for her bus, and soon she was turning her key in the lock. Slowly though, in case any of the neighbours had seen her and wanted a word. They never had, but you never knew.

She tried to be nonchalant about this arrival into emptiness. She put down her jacket, kicked off her shoes. It was Friday night so she went to the fridge, took out a half-full bottle of wine and poured a glass. Only then did she wander into the living room and glance at the answering machine. A steady red glow. Ah well. Even if there was a call, how many times had she felt the lurch of hope at the red blink, only to find it was a sales representative or a pollster? Who else would it be? The only person she could think of who might actually phone her was that girl from the office. And that was getting awkward. Last time it was a band somewhere over in Glebe. She hadn't been to a band for years. She didn't see how she could. And all the smoke. She'd said she had study to do. Which was almost true. It's something she'd thought about doing.

The flat wasn't the warm homey kind, not like those squat brick blocks of flats around Coogee, with their high ceilings and woodwork. This was modern, bright, airy.

But somehow she always thought of it as cool, almost cold. There was a small balcony though, where she could sit and catch a glimpse of the sea. It was good being near the sea. Walking by the sea alone was something you could do, without attracting attention. With a dog would be better, but she didn't see how she could manage a dog, all that looking after, remembering dog food, cleaning up after it, dog hair all over the flat. No, a walk by the sea. Nothing strange in that. She had noticed, however, that it was dog owners who stopped to chat to each other over their salivating mutts. There seemed to be a lot of laughter and swapping of telephone numbers. Maybe she should re-assess the dog situation.

Tonight was worse than usual. It was a long weekend. Perhaps the reason everyone on the bus had had a look of even greater eagerness. She thought, An extra day to get through, an extra night.

Tonight was okay. She was going to a play. *When I was a young girl I used to scream and shout*, was the title. She'd seen it in the paper. There was something about the title that tugged at her mind. Something about her country childhood, something messy that she knew she didn't want to examine. But plays were good. Even if you didn't really understand the whole thing. You could go along, look absorbed, come out and have a drink shoulder to shoulder with the chattering interval audience and no one would even notice you were there alone. She didn't feel so dull among these bright people. Sometimes she exchanged a smile or a word with the person sitting next to her. She would even ask to borrow a program now and then, just to say those words, have that interaction. Usually the person sitting next to her had a companion on their other side. Sometimes, she noticed, people held hands, or kissed, as if they were part of the performance.

Plays were good. Rides on the ferry were good, too. You might be a tourist for all anyone knew. Or going home. Or off to meet someone. And there was something about the harbour that let everything settle, so that it didn't matter if you were sitting alone.

One time, a man had come to sit beside her in the sun on the long seat down one side of the ferry, not far from the bow. He tipped his face up to the sun and closed his eyes. She noticed how dirty his jeans were and wondered if he was homeless. He opened his eyes and smiled at her. She panicked for a moment. Had he caught her frowning at the dirt-engrained denim? She tried to smile, but wasn't certain how it came out; it felt too tight, like forcing a spring. So she looked away at the water which sparkled enough to make that a likely thing to do.

Beautiful!

That's what he said. He said it in a breathy kind of way. She tensed.

He said it again, Beautiful. Isn't it?

She didn't look at him. He was talking about the harbour.

Yes, she said. She could feel him looking at her. The only thing about the ferry was that your hair could get very mussed up. Hers probably looked wild. She scraped at an unruly end.

Off to Manly for the day?

Yes, she said. To visit some friends.

After such a long sentence she couldn't not look at him. It would have been rude. He was smiling. She wondered at the difference about his mouth and hers. His seemed something so soft and loose that smiles must simply fall out of him.

You? she said. She wondered if that was what she'd meant to say, or if it was only the beginning of something longer. But she left it there as she found no other words attached to the first.

Me? Yeah. Going to help a friend. We're building a boat.

A boat. That would explain the dirty jeans then.

A boat? A yacht, you mean?

Mmm. A cat.

Cat?

Catamaran.

She said the word to herself. A lovely exotic word.

It made her think of romantic places, the Whitsundays, cruising and lying in a hammock, drinks on deck at sunset.

Oh.

She had wanted it to be a sound that showed interest so that he might say other delicious words like catamaran. Instead, it was dismissive, cool. She didn't know how to fix it. She sensed his mouth pull itself in as if with a drawstring. Why, oh why, did she always do this?

He got up, sniffed, raised his eyebrows and tilted his head in a gesture of farewell. She saw the Manly jetty behind him. They were nearly there. She uncurled her palm. It was almost a wave.

The idea of working with a friend on a project stayed with her. How long would something like building a catamaran take? You'd have to commit to every weekend, maybe even week nights. Perhaps there was something she could do – something she could build, or learn.

Home from Manly, she had looked carefully at the latest Adult Education classes. Even there, the commitment was usually ten weeks. She didn't think she could manage that. What if the phone did ring and there was a social occasion on the very same night? But she discovered that some classes were one-off. A single weekend, a day, an afternoon, even a couple of hours. It took a while for her to decide on one. At first she circled things like Introduction to Drawing, but was afraid she would turn out to have no skill. It would be too embarrassing. Card Construction seemed to hold less possibility for humiliation but was it beneath her? Who might do such a course? Pensioners. Desperate people. She circled a few courses she felt were for people like her. But did she want to meet people like her – the socially less adroit, the awkward? No. If she was going to bother, then she wanted to be among confident, happy people. She would do something exciting, but something requiring no skill. She would go on an afternoon exploration of the Sydney Harbour Bridge.

During the play, she remembered that the tour of the bridge was the next day, and was unable to concentrate on the rest of the performance.

The man in charge had a smile very like the shape of the bridge itself but upside down. She always noticed smiles. Her own cheeks twitched. He was a children's author, he said, but there was no money in it. So he took tours over the bridge as a day job. For my bread and butter, was the way he put it. His arms were strong in their easy T-shirt sleeves. How brown they were. She imagined him at his desk, writing longhand, the muscles in his forearm contracting with the movement of the pen. Or would he use a computer like she did at work? Surely not. When everyone else had told what they did, she said

Personal Assistant, and people nodded. There was a woman lawyer on holidays from Coffs Harbour, a young Canadian couple, four loud middle-aged Americans.

It had taken her hours to decide what to wear, especially on her feet. They said loose, comfortable clothing and sturdy sports shoes or walking boots. She got out the Blundstones she'd bought on holiday in Tasmania. She hoped someone might notice and she could tell them about her trip there. How all the tourists were couples. But meanwhile there were other things to concentrate on. He was explaining how high up they would be and how important the safety equipment was. They would all be linked together. He began placing harnesses over people's bodies. She was last. The others were keyed up and impatient. She had to stop herself from turning and running. He passed his hands gently over her shoulders as he straightened the webbing straps, smoothing, tightening. She could smell him, he was so close. He smelt like sunlight on fresh sheets. She bit back a sudden pressure of tears. It was a long time since anyone, any man, had touched her.

There was no time for anyone to ask about her Blundstones. She was up where she never imagined she could be, up on that iron framework which was only ever above. She was walking on the girders that the builders had walked on, that the painters walked on. She was looking down through the triangles and oblongs of gridwork at the water and the city as it receded. The air was getting thinner. She didn't feel scared. She was linked by strong fibres to the person in front and the person behind. There was something almost relaxing about it, she had set the ball rolling and there was no turning back. She felt lightheaded. She didn't feel like a Personal Assistant. It was as if all her clothes had fallen away to reveal that she was a magical creature, something gleaming, perhaps with wings. She leaned out to one side and was quickly pulled into line by the children's author. Not a place for going off the rails, he'd joked before they started out. Was that really a suitable sense of humour for a children's author? When they got to the highest point and stopped, she had the sudden thought that this was where people came when they did go off the rails. They stood here and contemplated, or maybe they didn't, but anyway they did what they came to do and took that final step into the unknown. She tried to imagine how it felt to have nothing left to live for. Not like her. She was thankful for her job. She was, after all, *senior* Personal Assistant to a quite important executive in a middling kind of firm with a downtown address. And for her flat. Perhaps she would get a dog after all. A small one. With the bark already taken out. Did they do that?

The children's author said her name, quietly. She

came back to the present to find the others all looking at her. It will be okay, he said. Of course it will, she thought, and wondered why they were looking at her like that. Something slid off her cheek. She looked up to see if water was dripping but there was nothing above them but blue sky.

Afterwards they went to a pub, somewhere in The Rocks. She felt like an angel fallen to earth, slightly ethereal, as if it wasn't blood in her veins but something much lighter, more silver than crimson. The others chatted and exchanged stories. She smiled. They seemed wary at first but then pushed back their chairs to make sure she was included. She didn't feel the need to contribute. What would be the right thing to say?

Suddenly, though, the children's author pulled his chair closer to her and looked into her face.

You okay? he said in a voice meant to exclude the others who were still huddling, talking.

She sipped a mouthful of her lime-and-soda and looked at his face. It was so clear that it reminded her of that open sky above the bridge. His eyes were blue, too.

I enjoyed myself, she answered, nodding. She thought all of a sudden that a children's author must have children. Why else would you write for them? She darted a glance at his ring finger, which was bare and all the same smooth brown. Not that it meant anything. Few people wore wedding rings these days even if they were married. And who got married? Mostly people moved in together. Lived together. What a difficult concept, living with someone. What if the other person was vegetarian? Or wanted to get rid of the television? Or ate different things for breakfast?

She pictured him at home eating breakfast. Somehow his mention of bread and butter had her imagining a slice of buttered bread cut into quarters, on a plain blue plate. She cut it further, into strips, bread soldiers. She placed a small child in a high chair at his side. The man was attempting to persuade the child, a boy, to eat up the rest of his boiled egg. The boy shook his head obstinately. The author dipped one of the soldiers into his own egg as an example. Somewhere offscreen, a baby cried. Offscreen. She had constructed the image in her head, like a film. Made it up. And now she believed in it. What we see, we believe. She believed he was a family man. But she'd heard it said you couldn't even trust photos anymore. People tampered with them, edited, added. You could do anything on computers. She next pictured him tucking the boy into bed and lifting one of the brightly coloured children's books he'd written. The boy's eyes closed gently as his father read in a hypnotising voice.

The voice was for real. He had been talking. To her. Now he was regarding her with some concern.

It affects people like this sometimes, he said gently. I'm not sure why. Overwhelming, I guess.

Photoshop. She recalled the name from some half-overheard conversation at work. Trumped-up shots of people in all kinds of compromising situations. She was not thinking compromising. She was thinking homemaking. She determined there and then that in the next term of Adult Education she would take a course in Photoshop. She would create a family for herself, slowly of course, beginning with a partner. She imagined the photos in her head. Smiling, holding each other, pregnant. She would send the photos, via email of course – or perhaps she would have a website where she would post them – to her family back in the country. They would stop worrying about her, stop nagging her to return home, find a nice farm boy, settle down. She'd tried telling them she was happy, that she was a city girl now, independent and free. They'd never believed her. Now they would see it with their own eyes. She would download the images and pop them in frames around her apartment. She would . . .

Perhaps another drink? he suggested. Or, if you like, I live not far from here. You could come back for a bite to eat. It's only a small flat . . .

Thanks all the same, she said. She hid a shudder at the thought of eating with young children, a baby even, mashing up food and dropping it everywhere.

But I wonder, would you mind? she said. She took out her camera. Didn't get to use it up there, she said.

He laughed. He leaned away slightly and angled his face towards her with a grin. Perhaps someone had told him it was his best side. His wife? Perhaps he did lots of publicity shots for his publishers. She didn't mind. She smiled. He'd be off home to his kids any minute. And she, first thing she got home, would be doing a search for that Adult Education guide. She was pretty sure she'd spotted a one-day course in Photoshop. Almost certain.

Losing faith

The first kick connects with my lower abdomen; the next blow falls on my ribs. I shift awkwardly, attempting to stem the onslaught. There is a wallowing movement within akin to once waking to a small earth tremor, my bed suddenly hammock-like, and the sickening instability of everything I'd believed in.

The baby stills. I try to make myself comfortable again, tweaking pillows behind my back, shoving one between my legs. There is not much room in the bed for the three of us and my bolsters. I think nostalgically of past insomniac nights when I could finally turn onto my stomach and drift off to sleep, thankful briefly for small breasts. My bible says that after week twenty-four, sleeping on your stomach feels like sleeping on a basketball. Try it sometime.

I lie thinking about the bible. *What To Expect When You're Expecting*. Expectations have been my trouble. Where is the chapter on disappointments?

I somehow manage to reach my watch on the bedside table without tipping off the bed. The word wallow comes to mind. I know exactly the feeling of the beached whale attempting to refloat itself, trying to thwart gravity, and thereby prevent its bulk from crushing its organs. Two twenty. I'm wide awake. I could get up and make myself a raspberry leaf tea. Or chamomile. Or read the Bible.

Snores from the other side of the bed make my decision. Have you ever heard a child trying to suck the last drops of a malted milkshake through a waxed-paper straw? With one arm I lever the top of my body from the mattress, then swivel the remainder around. I rest. Shuffling my feet into slippers, and dragging on a dressing gown which no longer closes across my overblown body, I traipse down the hallway to the kitchen. I push the door closed so my nocturnal foray won't disturb the peacefully snoring sleeper.

From habit I turn on the radio at the same time as the kettle. It is a program about spirit. Soul. Mystery. In the hush of two twenty in the morning the voices resonate as if in a church.

Pilgrims are making their way to a town with an Aboriginal name where the face of Christ has appeared on a wall of the local parish church. Priest and spokesperson, Father McGuire, says it is a true miracle. Not only the apparition but its timing, just when parish mass attendances were at an all time low. Now the church is bursting at its stone seams as the faithful come to witness this phenomenon which is surely a sign. A sign of what, Father? asks the interviewer reverently. That the Lord is watching. That He takes an interest in our small doings. And what do you say to those who scoff and call it rising damp, Father? They are unbelievers, he says.

He might as well have said, They are the damned.

I belong to that group. If the pilgrims belong to the faithful, then I am one of the unfaithful. I have no faith.

Yesterday I read in a newspaper that recent research shows regular church goers live an average of seven years longer than non-attenders.

If you believe, you live longer.

It's hard to say when I lost faith. Or if I really had it. Can a child truly have faith? Or does a child simply absorb the kit and caboodle of words, beliefs, superstitions, prayers, rituals, hopes, to the extent that if she were opened up in spiritual surgery they would all be found there, whole and undigested, like Jonah inside the whale? Perhaps I merely regurgitated the unpalatable and embarrassingly naïve chunks of religion once they became no longer obligatory.

But I fear a residue is left in the gut. In planes, I find myself beginning a Hail Mary. Even an Our Father. When I wander into cathedrals in faraway countries,

I genuflect, make an automatic sign of the cross and whisper. This although I often have no inkling of the church's actual denomination. If someone says, In the name of the Father, the Son and the Holy Spirit, I say Amen.

Wholly Spirit is the name of the radio program. Now a man is talking about his visitation from the Lord. The Lord came and stood right in front of him in the prison cell, just by the enamel sink. He was attired in white robes and sported a beard, a bleeding heart, stigmata. The man says he had no trouble recognising who it was straight away. The Lord told the man he was on the wrong path and must turn over a new leaf. And he must save not only himself but others as well. A tall order, particularly inside a prison, but the man had little else to occupy him. He discovered a purpose for his life and became a preacher. Out on parole, he now teaches people about right and wrong, drawing heavily on his own life for examples.

The raspberry leaf tea has steeped for long enough, and I add honey to temper the taste. I'm no longer certain I want it to do its job of softening the cervix, toning the uterus for its imminent exertions. I would like to stay in this state of suspended animation indefinitely. The urgency and excitement have disappeared since the magical due date has come and gone. And since I've begun to suspect I'm the only one excited about its advent. It feels as if this long-awaited, life-changing event might never happen, that it was all a lot of hype and hot air and that this is the anti-climactic aftermath. I've never heard of a phantom pregnancy which continued for the full forty weeks, but I suppose it could happen.

From the radio now emanates a spiritual tune, something between whale song and Andean pipes. My baby, phantom or otherwise, sways in time with the music, and I drift into a pleasant state of semi-being.

Next door's dog begins to bark. This has happened for the last three nights as the moon approaches being full. The dog – usually so quiet that I will pop my head over the fence to check he is still alive – barks and howls in the direction of the moon, as if calling to a long lost love who resides there. In recent months I have felt extreme irritation about this country music lament, as I've lain in bed attempting another short span of sleep before bladder, baby gymnastics or numb shoulders fragment my night. But tonight I feel a deep empathy with the hound and a strong compulsion towards the night outside.

I unlock the French doors and step into the courtyard. The air is shining. My lumpy moonshadow angles across the flagstones and up the retaining wall. I am bent at extraordinary angles. Now I understand my awkwardness. The dog intensifies his efforts. I imagine him sitting like a comic-strip canine, lips funnelled towards that piece of sunshine-reflecting rock which circles our own familiar lump of matter. The two pulling on each other. The moon pulling everything towards her. Us pulling back. No one getting the upper hand. No upper hand to be got. My vaguely recalled periods used to coincide precisely with the full moon, regular as clockwork. You could set your womb by it.

I lumber up the garden steps seeking the source of all this moonshine in a gap of sky amid treetops. There she is, sailing serenely among skimpy clouds. It is hard to believe man has ever trodden on her.

The moon is still one night away from full, and something about her misshapen roundness chimes in my own unevenly moony body. There is an irresistible tugging in my larynx. Small noises begin in my throat. A tentative humming emerges. It grows. The dog yelps and doubles his effort. I moan in time with him, disguising my lunacy beneath his instinctive yowls. Moans become howls and I really let rip. Up and down the block, dogs take up the cry. Lights come on in the few houses I can see between trees. Moon-calf, I think. I laugh and run for cover in the kitchen. Danny is standing inside the French doors.

What the hell are you doing? he asks, his whole body looking as pinched as his face, with a tracery of pale lines from rumpled bed sheets spreading like stretch marks across his distended stomach.

Having fun, I say. Being emotional, I add. Howling at the moon, I throw in. Don't worry, it's all in the book, all perfectly normal at forty weeks plus.

You'll catch your death, he says yawning.

I wonder what it would look like? I say dreamily, my mind conjuring small black angels wielding miniature scythes and me chasing them with a butterfly net.

You're mad, he says heading back towards the bedroom.

I gaze at his retreating naked back and buttocks as he waddles down the corridor. I tell myself I must have been mad to suspect there was something going on with him. What I mean is with him and someone else. Who would be interested in such a homely body housing such a lack of imagination? To say nothing of emotional distance. He is about as warm and nurturing as that distant moon, as unreadable and secretive as its dark side. Which is what aroused my suspicions in the first place. But now I realise that is just the way he is. They say your eyes change shape when you're pregnant. Perhaps mine have got bigger and I've finally seen something I've missed all these years. It astounds me that the energetic and bubbly baby inside me is half his.

I know it's childish but I stick my tongue out at his

diminishing back and hope he'll turn. He doesn't.

The Andean whale song ends and is replaced by the signature tune of the hourly news. I am a little afraid that it will be the first tune my baby hums in her crib, followed by serious babble dotted with unnatural stresses. News-punctuated radio programs have been my life-line to the outside world these last weeks. But I don't really want her to hear that East Timor may well be the next Vietnam, that beheaded bodies are being found down wells, that atrocities are being uncovered at every turn. The man who had the visitation and is now preaching on right and wrong will have a field day.

Nor do I really want my baby to hear that local police are stepping up patrols for today's coincidental – and in their opinion dangerous – occurrence of a full moon and the AFL Grand Final. The police are also expecting. Expecting the worst. Hospitals are expecting a ten-fold influx of casualties and are concerned they will be too short-staffed to cope. They fear that from this afternoon onwards resources will be stretched beyond the limit, that patients will not receive the usual standard of care, that doctors will work extended shifts and be exhausted, that nurses will be run ragged. They fear that mistakes will be made.

When I turn the radio off, silence sounds in my ears like a distant siren.

Shortly the siren becomes a reality, ambulance or fire engine I can't tell, but it's coming our way and next door's dog starts up again in response. Others join in. I've read it's to do with the frequency and their range of hearing. Over sensitive, I suppose you could call it. Nearly drives the poor things mad.

I decide to read for a while. The question of how to do it in some degree of comfort presents itself. Sitting up is not an option. Lying on already compressed shoulder bones is out. My belly in the beanbag with my book on the floor may be the only possibility.

Despite its physical comfort I've never felt emotionally at ease with this solution. I imagine my baby puzzling over sudden darkness replacing grainy pink light as she is enfolded in polystyrene furniture. The darkness of those horror-filled Timorese wells invades my mind. I shake it off. Don't entertain negative thoughts, says the Bible. Easier said than done. What? he'd stormed, his face contorting, when I'd tentatively asked, suggested. You're hysterical. Your hormones are making you hysterical.

Hysteria is named for the womb. That's if you have any faith in etymology.

Someone once told me that if you catch a child at just the right stage, emerging into language but still close to the birth experience, the child can describe the experience of the womb. I asked a friend's son and he told me unhesitatingly it was pink and smelled of onions. I remind myself to ask my own child. That is, if I'm brave enough.

I fall into the beanbag and realise it is the second most comfortable place for my body these last weeks. Number one is the swimming pool, where I drift in blue weightlessness, sounds distorted through water in my ears, light through closed eyelids. I imagine my own floating body and my baby floating inside me. In her smaller, amniotic world, sound and light are further muffled. Her clearest sounds are those my body makes, a strange symphony of unglamorous fugues to accompany my baby's twenty-minute bouts of sleep and wakefulness.

My own nights, I realise, have also become bouts of sleep and wakefulness. Happiness and disappointment. Joy and fear. Something and nothing.

What will I read? Three options present themselves – a book called *Science For Non-Scientists* which I'm reading to stop the rumoured deterioration of a pregnant woman's brain into a couple of handfuls of grey mush. This book tells me that's exactly what it is. It tells me many things about brain chemicals and hormones and why we feel the things we feel. Knowing doesn't help.

I could read the last chapter in the Bible, I suppose – the one on bringing baby home. I've never got around to that part. I haven't even packed a bag for the hospital according to instructions. He said he'd like to take care of that – something tangible, something useful. He hasn't, though. How will I manage without the maternity pads, winged, the post-delivery tracksuit, the phone card to herald the news?

I could examine the Bible's index to see if there is a listing on disappointment over nothing turning out the way you hoped.

There are chapters on erotic candle-lit hours with your loved one oiling the sensual tight mound of belly. There are pages on baby-safe exercises to do together. The delights of late-pregnancy sex are listed. Emphasis is given to time spent holding, touching, cuddling, enjoying, planning. These tenets have been absorbed inside me and if I were cut open in illusion surgery they would all fall out, untouched, untried, abandoned.

What do I do with the residue in the gut? I oil my own stretched skin daily, give myself orgasms slightly less often, swim three times a week, exercise at classes called pregnastics. Gestation. I am no longer surprised there is such a strange word for this experience.

Thinking of gestation, I wrench runaway thoughts to the third option – my novel-in-progress. A hackneyed parallel, the baby and the book, but I can't help myself. Long, painful, pre-occupying, joyous, distracting, maddening, overdue. From my noisy beanbag nest, I see the dog-eared manuscript poking out from under the sofa. I inch around towards it, using the basketball beneath me as a pivot.

Like the baby, it is finished. But it isn't ready. I turn pages distastefully. Again, I wouldn't mind this finished-but-not-ready state continuing forever. I cannot bring myself to put one more particle of energy into the book. Or into this pregnancy.

But my science book tells me particles of energy are unpredictable things and, although I begin lethargically, I am soon paying attention. I pivot again to find a pen and begin editing lines. I come across the word faith, and it suddenly strikes me that this is a possible and appealing name for a girl.

We have one short list of girls' names in a file on the computer. There are cobwebbed names from two generations ago, hippy names for fun, a couple of writers' names. Until now there has been none for an abstract idea. Something this child might bring with it.

I want to add the name Faith.

I wriggle and roll until I am free of the beanbag and go to sit at belly length from the computer, where psychedelic fractals disappear into themselves. Watching is like falling into infinity.

I don't know how long I sit staring but when I

come out of it my movements are slow and dozy, my hand inaccurate on the mouse. I accidentally open one of Danny's folders. The name of a file catches my eye. RELIGION AND ORGASM, it shouts. Precisely what I've been pondering tonight. I am intrigued. I open it.

Ten minutes later, I cannot operate the mouse. My hands are shaking so much I am afraid they will knock the computer to the floor. Four hundred erotic letters to a woman I've never heard of. Some of them planning, or recounting, assignations in sickening detail. A few even borrow my own special words of love.

Religion isn't mentioned in any of the letters. Nor am I.

As I sit shaking I feel, almost hear, a ping. For a second it puzzles me. Then a whoosh of liquid gushes over the computer chair and my thighs, down my legs, into my slippers and onto the Persian rug. I clutch the desk. I hear a voice as if from far away calling to me, HAVE FAITH. My lips begin to move. Hail Mary full of grace, the Lord is with thee, blessed art thou among women, and blessed is the fruit of thy womb.

Surprise, surprise

My face aches. Don't laugh. I mean that quite literally. It aches. Particularly across my eyebrows and in the area of the third eye. The stress, the pain of seeing too deeply with that eye? I don't think so. I don't look deep. I keep my gaze on the surface of things, catching reflections, noting shapes and shadows, averting my glance from insight. No, it couldn't be the third eye. I thought for a while that it might have been some nasty clinging thing growing behind my face, attached to my brain, invisible but menacing. There are other symptoms that could lead me in that direction if I let my thoughts wander and, after all, my mother had one, gnawing away, getting fatter, getting the better of her, gloating over its pride of place, right between the hemispheres, left and right. It got her in the end.

I recognised the true cause recently and it is this. My eyebrows, and they are heavy, and the whole of my forehead, are constantly straining heavenwards, into my hair, climbing towards my scalp, out of surprise. That's what it is, surprise. I go through life in a state of surprise. Shock. Not that life is constantly new, a procession of novelty. I take that back. In fact, life *is* constantly new, breathtakingly so, in its detail and ability to change and adapt. *And* it's a complete surprise that there *is* life. An accident. A one in a many billion chance. Not good odds. And maybe it just bounced off Mars anyway. But, as I said, I don't look deeply. I'm not a scientist or a philosopher. I live where most of us live, in the thin realm of our own reality. But I mean *my* life. In my life there's nothing much new, and yet, even there, I'm constantly surprised.

Take the other week, for instance. I was cleaning under the bed, finally, having seen thick wads of felted dust and hair poking out at the sides. And, lo and behold, I found a lipstick, a bright red one, so glossy. How do they get that sheen? I wondered. Not whale oil these days but possibly oil from some less recordable animal. And the smell. There is something very distinctive about the smell of lipstick. It goes straight to the amygdala and plucks an atavistic chord, whether it is the musk smell of rutting animals or the overpowering olfactory hit from childhood bathrooms, watching the mirror, your mother pouting and stretching her mouth wide, changing before your eyes into someone dramatic, unknown.

Anyway, bright red it was and not mine obviously. With eyebrows like mine, glossy red lipstick, or any lipstick really, would make the drag queens down the Cross turn to double-check. I was surprised. The dust had been there a long time, I admit, but I did dimly recall cleaning under the bed soon after we moved in. I asked my boyfriend about it. Well, actually, I left the lipstick on his pillow so he had to ask me about it. He said it must've belonged to the cleaning lady. Again, I was surprised. My eyebrows shot up dragging all the muscles of my face with them and some in my neck and shoulders as well. The cleaning lady? Do we have one? We did, my boyfriend reminded me, a while back. And it was true. I'd forgotten. I was surprised that I'd forgotten. But then she only came for two hours a fortnight and the arrangement didn't last for long. A mousy kind of girl, I thought, who kept her head down and vacuumed vigorously and in an enviably efficient way. I tried to be out when I knew she was due. My boyfriend took care of the money side of things with her. Yes, yes. Now I was less surprised that I'd forgotten and my forehead dropped accordingly. Ah, relief. Well, that explained it.

Then another surprise a few days later. My friend Susie ringing out of the blue and asking did I want to have lunch. I must be feeling a bit blue. No, I said (surprised), I'm feeling terrific, but I'd love to have lunch. Oh, I'd forgotten how good it was to have a long lunch with a girlfriend and I was surprised to find that I'd missed it without realising it. We went to an old favourite lunchtime hangout where the waiters are so relaxed they refill your wine glasses even when they've put all the chairs except those at your table up off the floor ready to clean before the dinner trade. We must've sat there four hours altogether and drunk two carafes of house red. I thought Susie had an expectant air, like she was waiting for me to make an announcement of some kind. Maybe she thinks I'm thinking about marriage, or a baby, god forbid. She asked a few leading questions like how things were with the relationship and was I happy and left spaces in the talking that I couldn't fill. I'm a bit surprised. She knows we're as solid as a rock. No worries there. I was keen to tell her about my new job, how I was loving it, all those books around me all the time, meeting people, a decent discount, no stress. She was envious and said, One can't have everything. Now what did that mean? She's doing very well – her own business, designing other people's interiors. She works with surfaces, too. They're important. People spend a lot of time on them. Take me and the books I sell. It's more the way they look and feel than anything else, the alluring print on the front, the smooth binding, the weight in my hand. That's what gets me in. Needless to say, I'm often surprised when I begin to read and find the contents don't match up to the hype on the dust jacket or the finesse of the cover. And Susie's clients care more about the particular shade of jade or avocado they have on their walls and whether it will clash with the ripened wheat covering on their sofa than whether the floor joists are sound. Life's too short to go too deep, but even at surface level there's a lot to surprise.

Something is niggling me about that lipstick, tugging at neurons even as I price glossy covers and squeeze books onto jammed shelves. Biography. Cooking. Decorating. Perhaps that's what it's about. Decorating. I don't decorate myself, really, for all that I like surfaces. But then you can't make a silk purse out of a sow's ear. Why try? Still, many women wear lipstick, make-up, have their hair done. Who for? I wonder. After work I look at all the women I pass in the street. A lot of lipsticked mouths hurry by. That particular shade of bold red doesn't seem to be popular, though. I don't see it once. I'd know it if I saw it. Suddenly, I stop in my tracks. The person behind me, a man in a suit, walks into my back and someone runs into his pinstriped back, treads on his heels and makes him swear. A veritable pile-up on the footpath. I say to the man in the suit, Our cleaning lady didn't wear lipstick, ever. She was a mousy thing in stretch pants and trainers. He looked surprised. I don't have a monopoly on surprise, I know. He caught me when I fainted. The man who'd trodden on his heels called the ambulance, apparently.

Yesterday at the hospital, they gave me the diagnosis. It wasn't surprise, after all, that was hauling at my facial muscles, tensing them like hessian ropes on a boat. That was just a story I told myself. One of my other stories was true, as it turns out. I always knew there was some parallel between my life and my mother's. I'd wondered if it might be that we got married at the same age. That would be next year for me. But, no, it looks as if the symmetry lies in the way we die. There is a little something, no, not little, but the size of an apricot on the scan they showed me, making my forehead feel like it's bursting, making my brow ache. Suddenly life is too short *not* to look deeply.

I told my boyfriend at lunch yesterday, broke the news. This morning I found an empty wardrobe and a note saying it was too much for him to deal with, I couldn't expect him to deal with it, could I, and he was going back to Melbourne to his former girlfriend who was waiting for him (and who, presumably, was free of troublesome tumours). I wasn't surprised this time. I'm over surprise. While I was in hospital I saw an article with a photo of his former girlfriend in a glossy magazine, saying she was in town promoting her latest film. She had just come from lunch with an interior designer friend. In the photo she was wearing a slinky black number, cut low at the front, and the most outlandish red lipstick.

Ceiling of an umbrella shop

Kunio slides back the glass doors of his shop and looks out. Other shops are still shuttered tight. Kunio likes to open early. He likes this time of morning before crowds come, when the peace and quiet of forest on surrounding hills seeps down into the street. Kunio has had this shop in the narrow street leading to the entrance of the Akiyoshido cave for five years now. He loves the street – its narrowness, the hawking of vendors, smells from fish fryers, orange carp turning in their cramped pond by the hanko shop. He loves the tourists with their cameras and expectant faces. He scans them carefully, even now, hoping against hope he might see the face he longs to see. For five years he has looked and he isn't about to give up now.

He loves his shop, too, for it is packed with things anybody might like to buy and take home to give to a loved one. A rice paper wallet, perhaps, stuffed with delicate writing paper and decorated with a woodblock of a woman in a flowing kimono at her writing desk. Or a box, lacquered and gilded, aching to hold precious things. Or a silk furoshiki to tie up something secret, a love letter, a ring. There are also mundane things, like boxes of local biscuits and fake lacquer dolls, trashy noren to hang on a wall for a week. And because the cave attracts geologists there are pieces of marble from the plateau, copies of fossils from Peru, gemstones from all over the world.

And there are umbrellas. Kunio couldn't imagine not selling umbrellas. He has sold umbrellas all his adult life and even some of his childhood. That was not here. That was in Kyoto, in a side street near Kiyomizu-dera temple, in his father's umbrella shop.

As he gazes down the empty street, it transforms into that other street below the temple. It is a spring morning. The city is filled with cherry blossom and visitors from every part of Japan. The narrow streets are crowded with sightseers. It is hard to believe a war has only recently ended. Behind him in his father's umbrella shop, a young couple are in the process of buying a parasol. They have been in the shop for over an hour and they have opened many umbrellas. The light is softened as it shifts through coloured rice paper. Kunio's father, Akira, is endlessly patient. Perhaps you would like to see just one more, Kunio hears him say for what seems like the hundredth time. Kunio is to bring tea for the couple and he walks quickly away from the shop down Sannen-zaka, in the direction of the Sakaguchi tea gardens.

The couple who own these tea gardens take pride in the traditional character of the place and Kunio loves going there. Perhaps there will be time for him to stop and have tea himself. But he remembers his father's customers and thinks better of this idea. Another time. At least he can enjoy the garden while he waits for the tea to be prepared.

He steps through the wooden gates and it is like entering another world. Plangent koto notes reach him in counterpoint to the trill of water running through split bamboo into the pond at the centre of the garden. A crane stands attentively at the edge of the pond, as still as a statue, though its eyes flick with the silver flash of carp. There is another flash from the corner of Kunio's eye and he turns in time to catch a glimpse of bright fabric disappearing behind the gate on his left. He keeps his eye on the spot and, after a minute or so, a small hand curves around the wood. Above the hand a lock of black hair emerges, then an eye, then the delicate face of a girl about his own age. He has never seen this girl before.

Hello, he says, I'm Kunio. Who are you? The girl steps out in her kimono as blue as the sky with a pattern of bright flowers overstitched with gold. She twists the stray lock of hair back into a knot at the back of her head. She stands straight.

My name is Ai, she says. Do you know what Ai means? It means love. I've come to work for my aunt and uncle. I've come all the way from Yamaguchi prefecture where we have the purest spring water in all of Japan. Have you ever been to Yamaguchi?

Kunio shakes his head, suddenly shy. He's never been anywhere outside of Kyoto. His parents are always busy with the shop. Besides, there was the war.

You must go one day, Ai says. Every drink from that spring will add a year to your life.

Then her name is called. She gives a slight bow and turns away. She hurries as best she can in her narrow kimono and wooden sandals.

Kunio orders tea and while he waits at a table in the garden he peers inside the tea house hoping to catch another glimpse of Ai. Perhaps she was a visitation, a vision giving him a message, not a real little girl at all. But then she appears carrying a lacquer tray with his teapot and cups. She puts it on his table and bows. Kunio blurts out, I work in an umbrella shop. In Sannen-zaka.

Ai smiles. She says, I shall be needing an umbrella. Then she makes another bow and goes inside.

It is four years before he sees her again. Although he visits the tea garden, he never finds her there. He cannot bring himself to ask. He goes about his work and studies his books but every once in a while, out of the corner of his eye, there is a flash of blue and gold. He catches his breath and turns but there is nothing.

There is no warning. He looks up from unpacking boxes of parasols and she is standing there. She is no longer a little girl but he knows her immediately.

I've come for that umbrella, she says and laughs in a way which puts Kunio at ease.

Well, he says, I don't think we'll have too much trouble finding one for you.

As it turns out, it takes them all afternoon. Kunio displays each umbrella, explaining in detail the process of manufacture, the quality of paper, the design. Ai holds them up, one at a time, and Kunio declares each one perfect. But Ai says, No I don't think so. Show me another.

Her aunt and uncle have kept her very busy and have sent her to school. That is why I haven't seen you, she explains, or come for an umbrella before now.

Kunio listens to the notes of her voice and afterwards can't remember the details she told him. Which school did she say? Has she finished now? Is she going to continue working for her relatives?

At last Ai says, This is the one. It is a parasol of dark magenta and is decorated with a kite trailing ribbons.

The kite looks so free, she says, but then you see the line of string and you know it isn't. She looks around the shop and laughs. Kunio looks and laughs too. The room is littered with open umbrellas as if they have blown there in a storm.

I like them that way, all open, Ai says. You should display them like that, so customers can see their design, their ribs, the texture of paper, as soon as they walk into the shop. Kunio realises that what she says makes sense. Together they begin tying and pinning and hanging and soon the entire ceiling is covered with open parasols.

They look like colourful mushrooms growing upside down, says Ai.

Or a sky of painted lily pads, says Kunio.

The roof of a Bedouin tent.

The painted roof of a cave.

Round river stones.

Round steps to a sky shrine.

Fruit of an umbrella tree.

The ceiling of an umbrella shop.

They are both laughing when the door from the shop to the adjoining house opens and Kunio's father steps in. He takes in the scene. The shop, a den of colour. The girl, her hair come loose from its clasp. His son, beaming.

We have a customer, he says bowing to Ai.

Yes, father. Miss Ai has decided on her purchase.

Kunio looks about for the parasol she chose but can't see it. Ai points to the ceiling. There it is, she says. We have put it up by mistake. Please would you mind getting it down for me? I must have that one.

Kunio's father nods. He almost smiles. He says, Very inventive, your display. Then he goes back into the house.

Ai and Kunio sit down on packing crates and laugh till there are tears. Then they stand up at exactly the same moment and, as if the hours and days and years have been preparing for this, they kiss beneath all that glory – the magenta, the crimson, the indigo; the kite, the blossom, the crane.

Someone calls, Good morning, in a scratchy voice and Kunio is suddenly back in Akiyoshido, at the door of his souvenir shop. Morning, he calls to the old woman who has a shop no bigger than an outhouse, where she sits all day carving tourists' family names into plateau marble. As if they might forget who they are, she says to Kunio one day.

It's going to be a beautiful day, adds Kunio. It's true. The sky is a pure brilliant blue without a hint of white anywhere. The air is crisp. It is the beginning of winter and there are often days like this, tender days when you can really breathe. Not many people visit the cave at this time of year, not the throngs of other seasons. It is a relief to Kunio. In summer, crowds are so thick this narrow street becomes a living creature, a many-headed serpent sliding and swaying, sloughing scales at shop doors.

It was like that the first time he visited the cave five years ago. He came to Akiyoshido, not for the cave of course, but to look for Ai. He had nothing to go on except the name of the prefecture. He thought, foolishly, that just by going there he might find her. When he arrived in the capital, Yamaguchi, one summer morning he stood at the bus station looking around as if he expected Ai to be there to meet him. But all the faces were faces of strangers. People were going about their day and whether it would be one of disappointment or joy was not evident. He planned to spend the summer in the prefecture, taking in the sights. At the same time he would ask questions and keep his eyes open. It was all he could think of to do.

One of the first places he visited was the spring near Mine. He looked into its translucent blueness and it reminded him of the blue of her kimono at the tea gardens that first day. He took up the wooden ladle and sipped. He remembered what she had told him about the spring water lengthening one's life. He sipped again. He might need a long life to find her.

Then one day he made his way to the cave. The bus took him through wooded valleys and small farms dotted with country houses. Farmers were working in the fields. He saw people cutting bamboo at the edge of the forests, chopping it into lengths and loading it onto bicycles or small trucks. Everybody had a purpose, it seemed. He too had a purpose but, unlike them, did not know how to achieve his goal.

He waited in line at the cave entrance for tickets. He felt in his pocket the trinket he had bought at one of the souvenir shops in the lane. A small umbrella. It made him feel better just having it there. Many of the sightseers were in groups and they huddled back in the shade of a wall while their tour leader organised tickets. So for some time Kunio did not see the cave map on the wall. It was only when one group moved off towards the cave entrance that he noticed it. It showed the various linked caverns, for it was a large cave, the largest in Asia it was said. Kunio stood reading the names of caverns until he suddenly gasped. One was called 'The ceiling of an umbrella shop'.

When he had his ticket he hurried into the cave barely taking in the dark gash in the rock face, partly obscured by overhanging greenery, the stream which poured from it and formed a pool before the opening. He pushed through the crowds, looking for the cavern.

He saw it in his mind – a ceiling of circles of rock with strata like parasol ribs. He walked the entire length of the cave without finding it. He walked back. Still he did not see it. He retraced his steps and thought he must be going mad. He saw signs painted with the names of other caverns but nothing about umbrellas. Finally he returned to the ticket selling office and pushed through to the front.

I'm looking for the ceiling of an umbrella shop, Kunio said to the uniformed woman behind the glass.

She blinked. He pointed to the map on the wall.

Oh yes, the woman said. That cavern can't be seen any more. There was a rock slide during the wet season two years ago which shut it off from view. A pity. It was beautiful. We kept meaning to change the map but . . . She shrugged her shoulders.

Kunio couldn't hide his disappointment. It was as if his only chance to find Ai had been shut off with the cavern.

I so badly wanted to see it, he said. Such a romantic name.

Yes.

I don't suppose . . . ?

What is it?

Is the name still on maps of the cave? Brochures? You know?

Well, yes, it must be. As far as I know.

Thank you. Thank you.

Now the street is busier. Shops have opened and tourists straggle by, looking into windows of restaurants and shops. The few tourist buses will begin to arrive later in the morning. Kunio keeps an eye on the street as he orders his display. He tries to give equal time to all of the shop but he is naturally drawn to the umbrellas. He opens them out and closes them, rearranges them for what he considers the best possible effect in the changing light of the day. He runs his fingers over their waxy surfaces.

After that day in the umbrella shop, Kunio and Ai met as often as they could. They would arrange to meet discreetly in the grounds of Kiyomizu-dera or Ginkakuji. They would wander temple grounds listening to the song of bulbuls and chickadees or the knocking of woodpeckers. Occasionally they would see a tanuki trundling into bushes and say it meant luck. Sometimes they met, apparently accidentally, on the temple-side walk called the Path of Philosophy. The secrecy was a necessity, for Ai was promised. A marriage was arranged to the son of a wealthy Kyoto merchant. Ai barely knew him. He was much older. She had no say in the decision.

They met through each of the four seasons, saw

blossoms fall and blow along streets, saw the rains come, the trees turn bright, saw snow soften the elegant lines of Kiyomizu-dera and temple ponds freeze over. Then one day Ai didn't come. Kunio went to the tea gardens and enquired. He was told the marriage had taken place. She now lived with her husband. As was proper.

Kunio filled his days with work. He made umbrellas more than his trade, he made them his passion. He waited to hear something from Ai but nothing came. Kyoto became a sad city for Kunio. He walked the Path of Philosophy and was aware of empty air beside him. He sat drinking sake alone at one of the small stands in Kiyomizu-dera's grounds. His eyes were alert for a magenta parasol but he never saw her.

After hearing about the fate of the cavern with the name which to Kunio was talismanic, he went back to the shop where he had bought the trinket umbrella. When they had chatted over the purchase, the owner had mentioned he was thinking of selling his shop to retire to his small farm. Kunio made him an offer.

Many years after Ai's disappearance Kunio heard a whisper that her husband had died and that she had gone back to her home prefecture. Kunio didn't know where exactly she was but he knew immediately that he would go and look for her. And that is when he bought the little shop in the Akiyoshido lane.

So far it has been fruitless. He has never seen her, or discovered anything about her. But here he can live in hope. In Kyoto there was none. So every day he opens the shop and scans the crowds. If she sees a map. If she reads the name. If she still thinks of him.

When the sun is high, briefly pulling the narrow lane out of shadow, Kunio walks along towards the cave to buy soba noodles for his lunch. He carries the tray back to his shop thinking of the day when Ai brought him tea on such a tray. He remembers the girl's face as clearly as he remembers the woman's.

He is so deep in the memory that at first he doesn't see the umbrella leaning against the wall next to his shop. But when he does, he knows it at once. The bamboo mat rattles on his tray and the ground tilts a little under his feet. It feels as if his heart has swollen up like a toad and is blocking his chest, his throat. He can't take his eyes from that umbrella.

Then a voice comes from inside the shop. I was hoping I might find a new umbrella, it says. That one is very old and I love it more than sleep, but I think I must leave it inside my house or it will fall into pieces.

Kunio puts the tray down carefully next to her

umbrella. He takes up the worn silver handle and opens the umbrella with hands so gentle he might be opening a woman's kimono. Along its ribs the paper is tearing away and there are patches where light streams through. Magenta has paled to the colour of sunrise and the kite trailing its ribbons is barely visible. The kite string has disappeared completely.

Emerald Princess

Kazuo follows the instructor's movements with ease despite not understanding the quietly spoken words which accompany them. It is not so much the foreign language as the fact that his one sense now far from perfect is his hearing. Old age, yes, but he also attributes this loss to his early proximity to far too much gunfire. Anyway he has always learned by example, by doing exactly as the master does, by copying. Not to mention that every single morning since he began school in the two-classroom building back in Okinawa he has completed a similar kind of exercise routine.

He finds that he likes this smooth-flowing Tai Chi more than the other exercises available, except for swimming. He still swims laps every evening following his afternoon nap. It wakes him up, refreshes him. On this trip he has tried yoga and also pilates. Both he found rather hard-edged, focussed on outcome, precision. But this movement is forgiving in its flow, allowing a certain personalised improvisation between one position and the next. He is just thinking that it is rather like writing with ink and a brush as opposed to a pen, leaving room for unique flourishes and ambiguities, when he finds he has followed the instructor to the end of the morning's series of movements. The instructor beams and wishes them farewell. *Au revoir,* she calls. *A demain. See you tomorrow. Same time, same place.*

You can't help but pick up a smattering of greetings and other politenesses in three or four languages on the ship. It is an American ship but the crew and staff are an international lot. Dutch, French, Polynesian, Australian. The captain is Italian and travels with his wife and two children. Imagine that! An endless vacation on the shimmering ocean. Kazuo had vaguely wondered how the children could possibly learn any useful discipline under such circumstances when he first heard about the arrangement. But the children were small and had their Filipina nanny with them. Perhaps discipline was not the highest priority. There is so much discipline needed later in life, he thought, allow them those few years of freedom. His own early years were a blank before the small school. After that there was so much discipline that he wonders how he and his friends ever learned to have fun.

Forgiving, yes. That is what he likes about Tai

Chi. It forgives him. There is room for mistakes, for imperfection. He begins one more cycle of movements for his own pleasure as the others move off in chattering groups. *Pool. Lunch.* More and more English words leap out at him now. It's as if veils are being pulled away from his mind. He comes back to centre with a graceful flourish and finds the instructor standing before him. She is very stylish, he thinks. Glossy short hair, lustrous skin and bright eyes. When she smiles at him, the already bright air on the covered deck seems that much brighter.

Ah monsieur, I still cannot believe it. It is impossible, what you tell me. Eighty-four years and you move with such grace.

She speaks English with a non-native speaker's precision and slower pace, and Kazuo is able to follow the gist. Grace, though. What is this grace?

Merci, he says to please her, to keep her smile lighting the air.

She laughs. *And* you speak French! There is no end to you, Monsieur.

She waves and walks off with a spring in her step which he now knows belongs only to youth. Grace, whatever it is, he might have, but that spring, like a young animal, never.

He ponders what the young Frenchwoman has said. He knows she was telling him that he looks younger than his years. People on this trip are always surprised by his age. At home, it is a different story. Many in his village are much older. Most. The young people leave. There is nothing to keep them. They head for the cities as soon as they can. They return once or twice a year, usually during Golden Week, for a bout of nostalgia and healthy eating to boost their dulled spirits and arm them with colourful anecdotes. In the city they tell slick new friends about their quaint home and its quaint folk. Outsiders now come more often than the children and grandchildren of the village. They come from all over the world to study people like Kazuo and his wife, Yumiko, octogenarians with the vitality of fifty-year-olds. Most of the village's population now consists of people eighty years and older, a number of them more than one hundred years old, though exact birth dates have not always been recorded and estimates of ages vary. These outsiders want to know the locals' secret, but the locals aren't aware they have one. They eat what they have always eaten, do the work they have always done. They often work together and always relax and socialise together. In the mornings, they do their exercises together. They have company and already more than enough stories to keep them going for a long time. They don't mind the outsiders following them about; it is something different, someone new to talk to.

Kazuo has no need to go back to his cabin. He is wearing the loose linen clothes he usually wears on deck. That is another thing he likes about Tai Chi. No sweat. It is as much about balance and harmony and quiet as it is about exercise and flexibility. Yes, the more he thinks about it the more he likens it to writing with his brush. It is as much about the act of writing beautifully as it is about the subject of the writing. He decides he will go to his favourite restaurant on the next deck for some fresh juice, papaya and something perhaps, and then look for Yumiko. He wants her with him when they enter the river.

There are four other Japanese couples on the ship. Only ten Japanese among three thousand passengers, a population greater than that of their village and the two adjacent villages put together. All five couples are retired, as are many on the cruise. They are no doubt doing what Kazuo and Yumiko are doing, spending some of their money before they die. It is a fine balance between spending and hoarding for them, since there is a good possibility they will live for at least another twenty years. But what else would they do with their money? They were surprised by how much had accumulated over the years. But after all, they worked hard and lived frugally. The money had saved itself. Being spendthrift does not come naturally to them. On Okinawa it is impossible to live the high life. And it would be beyond their reach to buy something like a holiday house, as real estate is too expensive for the likes of them. Anyway they are happy where they are, among friends, people who know them through and through.

It has been odd to find themselves among so many strangers after decades of living a sheltered life surrounded by people with whom they are intimate. At first they were astounded. They had flown with JAL to meet the ship, which was rather like travelling on a small metal-projectile-shaped piece of Japan. It was only when they boarded the ship it came home to them that they would be surrounded by westerners, chattering in other languages, mostly unknowable. Kazuo and Yumiko had not travelled. That is to say, Yumiko had not travelled and Kazuo had not left Japan since the war. The war had faded from his dreams over the years until he had thought he was free of it. But now as he grew old the dreams returned, more vividly than before. They brought with them a kind of restlessness, a feeling of something left undone. He doesn't say so to the outsiders who come, and would never say so to Yumiko, but he thinks that, with his memories of the war growing more vivid with each passing year and his regret increasing apace, another twenty years would be just too much of an ordeal.

He never spoke of the returned dreams to Yumiko,

but she knew something was disturbing the calm of their lives, not terribly, but irrefutably; she could feel it. It was like one of the many earth tremors which shook the sea bed around Japan. The islanders would always notice the unusual disturbance of the sea. It was partly to distract Kazuo that Yumiko insisted on the cruise. When they first stood in the shadow of the enormous *Emerald Princess*, her chest went tight the way it had done the time they visited Tokyo. She had not had any qualms about their trip until that moment, unlike her husband, who was not at all keen in the beginning. She brought him round to her way of thinking gradually. And the odd thing was that once he had accepted it he grew excited. He became animated about the journey. He had more energy, and his sense of restlessness was harnessed into preparations. Yumiko did not know that Kazuo had travelled this way before.

Over his juice, Kazuo studies the map of the Tasman sea. He traces their route from New Zealand. They are approaching Tasmania. He can feel a knot of anticipation growing in his stomach. He inhales deeply and exhales slowly, keeping himself calm in the way he trained himself long ago. He knows that most of the passengers will now be out on the decks searching for a first sighting of land. He was in his early twenties when he came to Tasmania. He shudders, instantly re-experiencing the pressing claustrophobia of the submarine. There was something about travelling underneath the sea in that metal pod which he found unbearable, even as a young man who was basically fearless. Fear, he has come to realise, increases as you grow older. He understands now why it is always young men who are sent to war. Not, as you might suppose, because they are the fittest and most able. They are not the most knowledgeable or the wisest. They are sent because they have not yet learned to value their lives, or the lives of others. They do not fear consequences in a deep way. They want to do daring things, adventurous things, they want to take risks. In a war, these desires are fulfilled to the *n*th degree. They have more than enough risk, and endless opportunity to pit themselves against danger or each other. Some of his compatriots were so young that they should have been at home competing in running races or ball games. Instead they threw themselves into battle with all the energy of the teenagers they were.

As a pilot, Kazuo was distant from hand-to-hand fighting. Face-to-face. At the time he felt good about that, more powerful, more effective, more objective. But the years taught him that the distance was a trick. The fact that he did not see with his own eyes the bodies and pieces of bodies, the screaming children, the blood, the devastation – all of these things inflicted by him – is not an excuse. It is an evasion. There is blood on his hands as surely as if he had used those hands to thrust in a bayonet.

His hands are sweating now. He lets go of the map and looks at his palms expecting to see traces of blood in the creases. They are brown hands, and worn by hard work beyond rough to silky smooth. They almost shine, but the lines and creases are deeply etched, deep enough to hide traces of treachery. Kazuo sighs and moves both hands into one of the smooth undulations of Tai Chi, a calm gesture of letting go.

I've been looking for you everywhere!

Yumiko is suddenly there beside him. Her face is the same shining brown as his hands, crinkled with her customary smile. Only her eyes show anxiety. When Kazuo brings his hands together at the end of the movement she places one of her hands over his joined ones.

Everyone is up on deck. We can see land. There are dolphins. Come and look.

Kazuo wonders if he has been wrong in not telling Yumiko. She knows him so well in every other way that it is as if part of him lives within her, deposited in her body and mind and heart. He suddenly remembers her as the girl she was when he came home. Seventeen, with the same smile, despite times which had been extremely hard. At least on the island they sometimes caught fish to eat. But others told him they'd had to become like the *habu*, the venomous island snake which can survive for two or three years without any food at all.

Yumiko had never asked for details of his time in the airforce. And anyway there had been a lot to do. The foreigners were there, occupying, overseeing, in charge right up until 1972. For all those years Okinawans were under American rule rather than Japanese. Okinawans had always been different and treated accordingly so were perhaps more accepting of this situation than others might have been. Yumiko learned more English than he had, deliberately working on making things easier for them. He had not had the will but had picked up some of the language anyway, mostly from Australians who came to buy fish from him. He never told them that he had been to their country, that he knew the contours of its southern coast almost as well as he knew the coast of Okinawa.

Eventually Yumiko opened a small restaurant which was popular with the Americans, and has continued to be a favourite of airmen from the Kadena American base even though it is out of their way. In the beginning Kazuo found it difficult watching his wife bowing and smiling and serving the Americans. But he was not in a position to lose face. There was nothing left to lose.

And before long he came to understand the fruitlessness of the entire war, of any war. He often thought of those four thousand men in the underground navy headquarters at Tomigusuku to the south of the island who suicided rather than surrender. If he'd joined the navy instead of the airforce like other local boys, he might have been among the suicides, instead of languishing in a camp. He'd had enough of the sea, he'd said. He was a fisherman like his father. He wanted something different, something exciting. He wanted to fly. And yet he had wound up spending much of his war in the sea, beneath it, surrounded, engulfed by it.

Up on deck, they stand side by side watching the dolphins' slow-motion rolls breaking the calm surface, their leaps. It reminds Kazuo of the performing dolphins at Ocean Expo aquarium on Motobu-hanto peninsula. He took his teenage great-grandchildren to see them on a rare visit a few years ago. They were bored by the show, preferring to listen to personal stereos or to thumb mobile phones. He remembers looking at them askance, thinking of himself at their age. The world was different and it was a good thing mostly. But how different was it really, when wars still raged around the world? Kazuo could not understand governments sending messages into outer space, searching for life there, when peace could not be achieved on this planet. What did they think they would do if they found other civilisations out there? Befriend them? Colonise them?

His eyes which, unlike his hearing, are still good – another thing those outsiders are always wanting to question him about – travel with the dolphins beneath the waves. He sees what they see. He follows them down, down to the sea floor. Most people imagine the sea floor as smooth sand but he knows, has seen with his own eyes, the contours, the cliffs, the sea mounts. It is a good place to hide a submarine, there among the sea mounts off Tasmania. Engine sounds and signals from the sub's instruments are blocked by the mounts themselves and by the teeming sea life which thrives among them. They hid there, like shy dolphins, after travelling on the surface in the night down the west coast of the island. For Kazuo it had been a great relief to surface, even though the danger of detection was increased. He breathed easily only if he could see the waves, the night sky and its stars. But when they dived to hide and wait, his temples pounded and his heart thumped along with the engines. He was a moth in a too-tight cocoon, encased, trapped, waiting for the release of flight.

It seemed to take forever for night to fall. They headed up into Great Oyster Bay and surfaced. If anyone, local fishermen say, had come across them on that moonlit night they would have disbelieved their eyes. What on earth? A giant bird attempting to snatch a giant fish, a whale, from the sea? A bird with broken wings? The submarine lifted on the gentle swell as the special crew worked to assemble the plane. The night was so still they feared the sounds of their tools would be heard in the settlement of Swansea across the bay. The lights of the township sparkled. No black-outs here. The townsfolk obviously felt no threat whatsoever, were oblivious to the fact that the enemy was so close.

There it is!

Yumiko is pointing. Ahead they see a bluish outline. Tasmania. They are bearing down on the island at a rate of twenty-two knots. Kazuo blinks into the bright light, his stomach clenching and his breath catching. Breathe in, breathe out, he tells himself. He pictures the estuary, its wide welcoming mouth, low hills on either side. To the west, the mountain looming over the city. A port city – fishing boats, yachts, merchant ships at its docks. Perhaps a navy vessel. The city itself tucked into the mountain's foothills, sleeping, innocent. The picture unrolls on a moonlit screen before his eyes. What is it he wants from coming here again? They were just young men doing their duty, living from moment to dangerous moment in the bright present, never pondering their role in history, in the slaughter of innocents, the expansion of an empire.

Yumiko places her arm along the small of his back.

Are you alright? Kazuo?

Kazuo looks down into his wife's eyes. Trusting eyes, they are. He leans down and kisses her on the lips, which makes her smile, knowing it is not something he would do in public at home. She has never had any reason not to trust him. But what would she think if she knew that Japan had once had designs on this outpost and that he was the one, one of the ones, who gathered the necessary information for that design to be worked?

The sea plane felt like a plane which had been put together in a few hours by a team under stress in cramped conditions on top of a submarine in the dark. It rattled and ran ragged. It didn't pay Kazuo or his co-pilot to think what might happen if a problem developed. Or to imagine sending a mayday radio message and ditching the plane in the sea. It didn't pay to imagine their presence being detected or how many anti-aircraft guns were in place. Probably – they had banked on this – there were none. Somehow these Australians saw themselves as impregnable on their large southern island. Darwin had been a shock to them. Broome took them by surprise despite the fact they must have known by then that the Japanese would come. And the mini subs had been prowling undetected for the longest time, dropping lone scouts and their radios on uninhabited coastlines to wander in the outback till they perished of thirst. Or simply gathering information – the lie of the land, defence preparedness. So far, Australia was looking like a pushover.

At the time, all of these things about Australia pleased him. It was like a game. A child's game. And it seemed that way because he was a child, or barely an adult. He was blindly doing the bidding of those who cared not one jot whether he lived to have children, died bravely or otherwise, was injured, debilitated, scarred for life. And why? This is what he asks himself over and over. Why was he agreeing? Was it youthful enthusiasm for the adventure? The opportunity to test his wings? And why was his country plotting an invasion of Australia? Whatever the reason at the time, none of it makes sense to the eighty-four-year-old man standing at the rails on the second deck of the *Emerald Princess*. Now, it is something other than gathering intelligence that he wants, but he doesn't know exactly what. There are no powers on high to tell him what to do. Perhaps merely returning will be enough to lay to rest his doubts about himself. Perhaps.

The *Emerald Princess* carries three thousand passengers. She weighs in at one hundred and sixteen thousand tonnes. She has five pools, nine restaurants, thirteen bars and two nightclubs. She is two hundred and ninety metres long with eighteen decks in all, making her sixty-three metres high. In other words, she is taller than most of the buildings in Hobart. She is too big to come alongside the wharf next to Salamanca Place. Instead she must tie up at a more distant wharf usually reserved for cargo ships.

There were five cargo ships in port that night in 1942. No warships. Beneath him people lay asleep in their beds, mostly women and children he now supposes, considering the men would have been away where the war was openly being fought. Sleeping, breathing gently, unafraid.

Kazuo is lost in thought at the railing, looking up at the blue mountain beyond the city. Yumiko is watching other passengers disembark and board small buses on the wharf. At each port of call, they have tended to hang back, and then to walk. They like to take their time and be independent. An engine coughs roughly into life nearby. Kazuo is roused from his thoughts by the familiar sound, and turns to look. Behind the ship, a sea-plane begins to taxi along the river, then slowly lifts into the air, its floats making it particularly bird-like. Kazuo watches it climb into the clear sky and circle over the river. They have been told what activities and attractions are available during their brief stay in Hobart. A joy flight, he thinks. Flying for the sheer joy of it. Imagine.

Later, they find themselves a few blocks back from the wharf. They have wandered through crowded Salamanca market, among sellers of everything from fruit and vegetables to second-hand wares to oil paintings. Yumiko has bought souvenirs for friends at home – kitchen utensils beautifully crafted from fragrant Tasmanian timbers, Sassafras and Huon pine. Kazuo cannot take his eyes from the faces. The happy, laughing, shouting faces. Children whooping and eating fairy floss. Adults touting, bargaining, enjoying themselves. They are safe, he thinks. They are alive. There was no invasion. No bombs fell. *But it is no thanks to me.*

They pass a squat sandstone church with a large billboard outside its open doors. Big white plastic letters have been slipped into place along metal brackets. DO YOU HAVE THE GRACE TO GO TO HEAVEN? Kazuo and Yumiko walk through the iron gate and sit on the grass with their backs to the sign. They are not sure if they are really allowed to do this, but the sign does not say, Please do not sit on the grass, and it is peaceful there. They have brought their usual flask of green tea. Anyone passing would smile at the elderly couple kneeling on the lawn with their backs so straight, holding small ceramic cups between their fingers and sipping delicately. But it is a quiet, dead-end street and no one passes. Kazuo stands up and stretches. He feels something loosening in his body. His arms begin the slow arabesques of Tai Chi. His legs follow. His spine bends and twists, sinuous as the *habu*. He is writing something significant with his body. When he comes back to centre and stills himself, he holds his hands out to Yumiko to help her up. She smiles at the man she has loved for sixty years. He looks like a man who knows what he wants.

The pilot of the sea plane is able to help Kazuo. Money changes hands and no more questions than necessary are asked.

The liner is due to make her stately departure at six in the evening. This way the passengers can enjoy the golden light of the late afternoon, the gentle sky. Well-wishers and the curious have gathered at the wharf to watch the huge vessel take her leave. They are not used to having a ship of such proportions in their midst. Passengers line the railings and wave to those on shore, friends and strangers alike. Kazuo and Yumiko join in. They laugh as they notice how their way of waving goodbye is different from nearly everyone else's, except for the children's. They wave like children!

There is a festive air. The couple standing next to Kazuo and Yumiko are from Hobart, having just joined the cruise. Introductions are interrupted by the deep bellow of the ship's horn blast which seems to echo back from the mountain. The others do not notice the sound of a small plane, but Kazuo's head is up, his eyes searching the sky. The others look up, following his gaze. Yumiko smiles at their new acquaintances.

Kazuo has not good hearing, she says taking care with her English, but always he hear planes before I hear. He was pilot long time ago.

The Hobart couple smile and nod. They shade their eyes and tilt their heads towards the plane. On deck and on shore people point upwards as a tail of smoke issues from the little aircraft and it goes into a dive. Is it on fire? Or is it a display of aerobatics? But no, it is writing something, sky writing. An excited murmur runs through the crowd. What fun! Probably a farewell for the *Emerald Princess*.

S! yells someone, as the letter is finished. The crowd takes up the chant. A soft white letter S stands against the blue of the sky. The plane loops the loop. O! is the next cry. So long? an American guesses. The plane climbs and plummets, its engine like a shrill voice rising and falling. R! they shout together as the plane rolls. And another R! They wait.

He's writing Sorry, the Hobart woman says.

Y! everyone shouts. SORRY! yell all the children who can read. It says sorry! A cheer goes up.

The *Emerald Princess*' turning manoeuvre is almost balletic to watch. She rotates slowly in the river. She sounds another deep and mournful blast of her horn, drowning out the crowd's cheers. Her engines go into forward and she heads majestically down river. The crowd gathered up by the Domain cenotaph has a wonderful vantage point. The view of the river and the departing cruise liner is nothing short of spectacular. Whistles and cheers follow the ship down the Derwent. The five letters high in the sky slowly grow larger as they thin out, then they disperse into the air.

Ice

He comes home on a red ship, carrying thousand-year-old ice and visions which keep him from sleep. He walks down the gangway reluctantly, holding a blue sports bag and a white cooler. The town's cosy tidiness slows his steps on the metal. What is there for him here after what he has seen? Even the mountain looks homely, like a giant dark marrow.

He can't see that all the trees up there bend low in one direction, forced into obeisance by icy winds from the south, can't see how trees peter out altogether above a cruel invisible line, beyond which there are threatening dolerite pillars and boulders strewn as if by a violent hand. He doesn't see danger; he is bedazzled by sunlight, moonlight, starlight on snow and ice, by miles of emptiness and clarity, and thinks all this tame by comparison.

His first thought is for the ice. He has to find a place fast where he can perform the ritual he intends. He steps from the iron walkway onto tawdry wharfside concrete. For a few moments he is unable to lift his gaze from its ugly greyness, its film of oil and tar and cigarette ends. It repulses him. He recoils. He steps backwards onto the gangway. Behind him voices rise in anger. What the fuck's the hold-up? Lost your land legs?

He closes his eyes and breathes in deeply, imagining pure icy air enter his lungs, sending invigorated blood scurrying around his body. He sees luminous ice all about him. But then a whiff of diesel and frying chips invades his trance and his blood becomes sluggish again. He sighs and steps onto the ground.

He casts a glance along the wharf where welcomes are various – tears, laughter, kisses – and he looks beyond to lights in the street which shine erratically, tantalisingly, the way the aurora did on good nights. His steps turn that way as if of their own accord. The sound of them is strange to his ears; he listens to his own footsteps as if just returned from the tomb, amazed by the solid thudding, then offended, wishing instead for the soft swish, swish, swish of his tread on snow.

Town lights blur together now as his eyes adjust to new light conditions. He shakes his head, scrunches his eyes. When he opens them he sees an angel.

Next to the seafarers' mission, where the blue angel flies indefatigably, is a pub. He directs his steps to the door and, since his hands are full, attempts to open it by leaning his elbow on the brass handle and his weight on the door. Used to the slow opening of heavy ship's hatches, he leans hard and finds himself on the ground. In fact, on the beer-and-cigarette-smelling carpet of the front bar. There is a lull in Friday evening chatter and patrons' glasses stall in mid-air at the sight of a very hairy man in bright outdoor clothes and big boots spreadeagled right inside the door. People usually fell out, not in. But by the looks of him he's been drinking. Isn't he carrying his own cooler, the top of which has come adrift on impact, and isn't there a quantity of ice strewn across the carpet? No doubt there is a bottle or two in there as well. A sly drinker, perhaps. Someone seeking the warmth of a pub on a Friday night but too cheap to pay pub prices for drinks. Then again, he doesn't look the type. Looks more like those blokes you see leaning impatiently on the foredeck rail of the red ship tied up opposite, waiting for the final stowing, the engine repairs, the right weather, waiting and waiting to be gone.

Nobody offers a hand. Every hand is full. Holding a cigarette, a drink, another's hand. He lies there with his senses assaulted by the sourness under his nose and wonders how he will survive. Then a glint catches his eye and without looking he recognises that special shattering of light. He scrambles for pieces of ice, scooping them up from the worn, dark carpet like large diamonds from velvet, and placing them carefully in their cooler.

People have begun to chat again, getting on with saying whatever becomes suddenly so important to say on a Friday night. Though some of them watch from the corners of their eyes, only one turns mascared eyes full on the spectacle, and her tawny eyes sparkle like the rocks of ice. Her lips glow, glisten red like fresh oil paint on canvas, and curve upwards into a smile which turns itself into a laugh. The woman, whose red dress matches her lipstick, lowers her high heels to the floor and holds out a red-nailed hand. He looks up at this vision of red and takes her hand in his big fingers, cold and wet from the ice. Heads turn a fraction towards the tableau. She gives a tug and the man and his cooler heave up from the floor. He is shocked by the strength in that small red body. He sits on the stool she pats. She climbs onto the next one and smiles at him. She takes a deep breath through delicate nostrils.

I smell ice, she says. On gold wires through her earlobes, chunks of Killiecrankie diamond swing backwards and forwards, backwards and forwards, and his eyes follow them longingly.

In Estonia, she is saying, we build ice sculptures for the New Year. Everyone comes out into the freezing night to look. There are lights around the ice and it shines enough to light up the night, as if the moon has fallen to earth.

His eyes are full of it – fallen moon and ice palaces. She can see them there; he understands.

His glass holds whisky. Hers, too. The moment is approaching. He lifts the cooler lid and places it on the bar. He takes out a chunk of ice. He places it with a clink into her whisky. He takes another piece and drops it into his own glass. They look at the ice bobbing in their glasses. They listen to it pop and fizz and splinter.

The air in that ice, he says, is a thousand years old. Perhaps it was once air in Estonia. Perhaps this water was once in a river in Estonia. Or France. Or Zimbabwe.

He lifts his glass and puts it into a spin of small circles with rhythmic shifts of his wrist. The contents of the glass swirl like a miniature maelstrom and ice melts into whisky. She copies him. They clink their glasses together and drink.

He feels it happen, feels time drain into him and flow through his limbs. Ages race through him and he feels the shift of continents, the movement of glaciers. He looks at the woman to see if she feels it, too. Her glass is empty and her eyes watery. He takes it for a sign that time is welling up in her, too. He is mistaken.

What wells up in her eyes is a longing for those ice festivals with brothers and sisters, a mother in furs and the music of her own language mixed in with the laughter.

Here, she says turning to him, I can't speak. No one knows my soul because I can't express it. If I talk of the ice festival, to you it is just two words, a phrase, a thing. To me the words are magic, swirling with colour and light, and my heart nearly bursts with the beauty of it all.

He sees the aurora swirling in dark sky. He sees the beauty of blue ice. He orders more drinks, changes his mind, buys a bottle and places it between them. He fills their glasses, lifts chunks of ice and holds them up to the light, the way a priest might raise the monstrance, then dumps them in their drinks.

She thinks of the one other time she told a man about the ice festival, its architecture of light, the cold beauty. The strange thing he said: Pull the other leg. The way she looked at him guardedly as his words unfolded in her mind. She did not know then what he meant or why he would say such a thing and she was too embarrassed to say so, too hurt. She had offered him her vision and he told her some kind of riddle. She had thought she would not tell another. The only thing she offered after that was her body because its language was direct and without riddles, and it made her feel less alone.

We see only a portion of an iceberg, he says. But the

mass you don't see is the most fascinating. Old layers of snow are compressed by new layers. Snow turns to ice. Deep ice, and the air trapped inside it, has been compacting for hundreds, thousands of years. It is extremely dense. When an iceberg breaks away from the ice shelf or glacier, it bobs around looking beautiful. But that deep old unseen part of an iceberg is incredibly dangerous. Sometimes a berg beaches and displays its deep layers.

She clinks ice against the side of her glass, listening to its splutter. His words blossom in her mind, reveal their meaning, and she knows, suddenly and without doubt, she is exactly that. She is an iceberg.

He is still talking. Antarctica is the only country which truly belongs to herself. She is beyond borders. Yes, we have laid our puny hands on her, staked our paltry claims, built our toy garrisons. But she is oblivious, magnificent. Her time is that of stars, not the tickety-tock toy-time of men. She is perfect.

Borders, she says, are what my country is all about. The gulf, the Baltic, Lake Peipus, and the giant at our back. These borders reach around my people's minds, corralling their thoughts.

When sea ice forms, he says, it appears like giant pale waterlilies. The ice pushes out most of the salt. Ice on top of the sea is almost pure water.

My people have mixed with the Russians. But still they are not truly mixed. They separate or are separated. They know about pure.

The bottle is almost empty. The cooler is already empty. Between them they have drunk meltwater from all the ice he brought back on the red ship. He sits brooding over the empty cooler.

She slides a delicate red-tipped hand up his thigh. Instinctively he pulls away, not wanting to sully the pure space in which he exists.

But in his body, he now feels an ancient force, something driven by aeons, and the urges of planets. He leans towards her and catches one of her twinkling earrings between his lips, then between his teeth, as if he will crush it. He breathes into her ear. He notices how perfect the ear is, certainly as perfectly formed as an ice crystal, but warm.

He thinks, She is my cure. She is the opposite of the pure untouchable maiden, Antarctica. She is flesh, warm, touchable, available.

She thinks, I am an iceberg. Spectacular surfaces obscuring compressed pasts, submerged danger.

Suddenly it is she, rather than he, who is reluctant. But she has not learned the art of prevarication in this stiff language. They go up the street, up some stairs, and into a room. On the wall is a photo of the red ship.

She stands looking at the photograph. In it, the ship appears to be marooned in a paddock of ice. Whiteness stretches in every direction, and the ship in the centre is as insignificant as a drop of blood on the skin of a human body. Or on a white sheet. Behind the ship is the path it has opened up, a path of bright water that the woman feels she could walk along. She would clamber over the stern of the ship unnoticed, stow away until the ship reached its destination and she, too, could come home with ice in her eyes.

When he touches her bare shoulder, he notices how cold she is. But there is no gooseflesh; her skin is as smooth and translucent as pearl. Through a gap in the curtains, it catches the light of the moon, shining up at him. He draws her cold body against his hot one, shudders at the touch of her against his chest, his stomach, his thighs. He feels her cold fingers on the hottest parts of him, groans at all he is leaving behind. Later he flows into her in a hot river and falls soundly asleep for the first night in fifteen, right there on top of her thin body.

It is never the same, though they are saying the same things, these bodies. Talking about need and loneliness and longing, not about love. Not until tonight when this man who is the first to understand her, wraps himself around her as if she might save him. When it is she who wants to be saved. Who wants to be loved. Yes, he has found her out, taught her to herself. He has revealed it; she is an iceberg. But he is the one to thaw her, uncover what is hidden. He is the one.

When he wakes, it takes some moments to piece together fragments of thought and know where he is. He is lying face down on a wide bed. The bed is soaked with his sweat. The bedclothes beneath him are drenched. He wriggles away from the dark wet patch. He remembers and looks for the woman. He calls out.

A sparkle on the saturated sheet catches his eye. He reaches out and, between his broad thumb and forefinger, lifts an earring.

Santa's little helper

Rosalind stares in amazement at the grand brick façade of the Masonic Temple. Until today she could not have said where the city's Masonic Temple was, but it turns out to be right where she usually parks her Golf when she goes to the Saturday morning Salamanca markets. And – this is the thing – she has never noticed. She has never looked up beyond the imposing wooden doors and huge stone plinth and seen the two-foot-high carved letters which announce this building's purpose. And, as the letters are in stone, it has clearly been this building's purpose from the word go. Well, well. You just never see things properly unless you walk. She learned that in Europe a long time ago. Always walking, seeing the detail in things. And then when Tom was small. They always walked a lot, she and Tom. And before long he was pointing up at buildings and crying S! when he saw one of those squiggly metal brickwork reinforcements, or Lion! if there was one, rampant, above a doorway on a coat-of-arms. She now recalls having been amazed by what he noticed, and appalled by what she herself missed. For instance, how often the phoenix appeared on buildings. Bird! Tom would say, pointing. His very first word. Not an auspicious symbol for a building, she would have thought. She smiles at the memory. She thinks, If god is indeed in the details and you want to know god, walk. She winces then, the thought of Tom suddenly turning painful.

The red, green and white balloons, which are bouncing in the slight breeze coming off the river, seem incongruous, tied as they are to the portals of this solid building. It's like an exercise in opposites, a page in a child's picture book. Heavy. Light. But the balloons tell Rosalind, loud and clear, that she is in the right place. The heavy doors are already open, great hooks slipped into iron loops in the stonework on either side. Still, you would not call it an inviting exterior, regardless of balloons. Rosalind hesitates. She turns and looks across the road towards the wall of St David's Park, which she has just walked through. It was unusually deserted today, of course, more like a private garden of a grand house. The streets, too, were very quiet, everyone at home opening presents, popping champagne. She has a book in her bag. A good book. She could cross the road, slip through the corner entrance into the park, find herself a comfortable spot in the shade, stretch out and read for a couple of hours. That would be pleasant. It's something she knows she would enjoy doing. But the trouble is, it's a public park. Which makes it so public! What would people make of a woman stretched out in the park in the middle of Christmas Day? Alone? Somehow, alone is not acceptable at Christmas. Alone marks you. You are without loved ones. Ones to love you, and be loved by you.

This train of thought is interrupted by a clearing of the throat. Rosalind spins around to see a woman about her own age standing in the doorway, her hands on her broad, red-and-green-aproned hips. What is striking about the woman is that she is also wearing a large pair of reindeer antlers. Very large. So large she looks as if she might topple over at any moment. They look, Rosalind thinks, as if they might actually be real. Rosalind stares at the reindeer woman as if she really might be some mythical beast, part human, part reindeer.

The woman's face, below the antlers, splits into a big smile. Are you here for Christmas lunch? she asks.

For a moment Rosalind allows the image of the book in the shady spot in the park to hold sway in her mind.

Yes, she says then. Yes, Christmas lunch. I hope I'm not too late.

Too late? Not at all, says reindeer-woman. We're still

setting up. Only a few punters so far. Perhaps you could give us a hand laying the tables?

Rosalind smiles. This is going to be easy after all. Of course there was always going to be a need for extra volunteers. Even volunteers who have left it to the last minute to make their availability known. She still doesn't understand why she has procrastinated for so long. She's known about the lunch for weeks now, having found the information on the internet. But she just couldn't bring herself to phone and make the offer. Something about it made her, what? afraid? ashamed? Sometimes it's hard to pinpoint emotion and give it a name. But whatever feeling it is, she has felt it right up until this moment. Now, everything seems as if it's going to be all right.

She steps up into the cool entry-way and follows reindeer-woman into a hallway with a gleaming parquetry floor. Someone has clearly applied a bit of elbow grease recently. Nevertheless, the interior strikes Rosalind as less imposing than the exterior, even though the scale remains big. Reindeer-woman's heels click loudly over the shining floor. In runners, Rosalind trails silently behind her like a poor cousin, or a thief.

I'm very fond of reindeer, Rosalind finds herself saying into the vast emptiness.

The antlers swing alarmingly as the woman turns to

glance over her shoulder. She looks a little startled, but then gathers herself.

I hope you don't mean to eat, she says with a smile. It's not on the menu today. We're pretty traditional here. She turns to front again.

No. No, I meant . . . Did you know their velvet is the fastest-growing tissue in the entire world?

Rosalind tries unsuccessfully to draw alongside the woman. The antlers project quite far to the side. Rosalind tries to get a good look, to see if they're real or not. Surely not. But people used to kill reindeer for just such a trophy.

Reindeer-woman stops at another pair of open double doors and turns back to Rosalind. Their velvet? she says. Rosalind pushes both her hands above her head in a branching motion. Reindeer-woman nods her head, and her antlers waggle at Rosalind. Rosalind giggles. Reindeer-woman turns away.

They enter a large hall crammed with long tables covered with white cloths. There must be seating for at least a couple of hundred. Rosalind is shocked. Surely there aren't so many people in this town with nowhere else to go for Christmas lunch.

So many? Rosalind says.

Reindeer-woman looks at her. Last year we fed three hundred, she says. This year it's likely to be more.

I had no idea, Rosalind whispers.

The woman looks a little more closely at Rosalind's stricken face and her manner becomes gentler. You'll be okay, she says. Don't worry. She gives Rosalind a pat on the shoulder and turns away again.

Small windows are placed very high in the walls of the dining hall but Rosalind imagines it must normally be rather a gloomy space as all the electric lights are turned on, even on this sunny morning. The room looks bright, festive. It has been decorated with red, green and white streamers, lots of silver and gold tinsel and all sizes and shapes of shiny baubles. A large fake Christmas tree sits in one corner, small coloured globes flashing intermittently, apparently at random. The effect, though, is of a wave of light flowing backwards and forwards over the tree. The emptiness of the air above all this colour and activity is what Rosalind notices. The ceiling is so high that the lines of long trestle tables are made to look quite small, as if they might soon seat a throng of dwarves. The tables are all deserted. A few people move among them with cutlery and glasses, laying out places. They are all wearing Christmas adornments on their heads – reindeer antlers, Santa hats, angel wings, elf hats.

Rosalind can't help it. She finds something desolate in all of this, something unnerving. This is what she was afraid of, she realises. That this might be worse.

This *fakery*. This semblance of a festive, happy, shared Christmas.

Reindeer-woman bustles on through the hall and Rosalind follows with a sinking heart. They turn into a large kitchen and suddenly the mood is completely different. This room is *alive*. People are everywhere, stacking plates, slicing meats, laying out trays of food, counting cutlery. There is a hubbub of talk and laughter. And what strikes Rosalind immediately is the range of people. There are white-haired men and women, dressed conservatively, and young women wearing low-slung jeans, showing bare midriffs. There are a few young men, too, and her heart lurches. It's as if, for a moment, she thinks she might see her son there among them. As if, all along, hiding it from herself, she has really come in search of him.

Rightio, says reindeer-woman cheerily. This is Shimal. He's laying tables and he could certainly do with a hand. Or twenty.

Rosalind, Rosalind says weakly, holding out her hand towards the black-skinned, black-haired young man.

Shimal smiles widely at her and pulls an apologetic face. His hands are hidden under a large pile of white plates.

It is very nice meeting you, Ms Rosalind, he says.

Rosalind puts her hand down, awkward.

Let's go . . . is it? . . . cracking, Shimal says now, laughing a rumbly laugh which makes the plates wobble.

There is a pause. Then Rosalind understands. Yes, she says. Cracking. That's it. Let's get cracking. Although . . . perhaps . . . She points to the stack of plates. Perhaps not a lucky expression, she adds.

Shimal frowns at her. Rosalind can see him thinking over her words. Suddenly, that big smile splits his face again.

Ah, yes, I see, he says. Yes, not lucky. It is very funny, Ms Rosalind.

The plates wobble again between Shimal's arms. Reindeer-woman has reappeared with a trolley. On it are piles of cutlery.

Here, she says. The trolley might help. Much more efficient.

Shimal carefully manoeuvres the stack of plates onto the trolley and sighs with relief. Rosalind follows Shimal and the rackety trolley into the echoing space of the dining hall. Shimal is clearly not certain how things should be laid out. Rosalind steps in and begins putting a plate down in front of each chair. She lays out the cutlery. Shimal follows suit, and together they work their way in silence along one side of a long table. Rosalind can't seem to find anything to say. She keeps thinking about where

Shimal is from. Somewhere in Africa clearly. Should she know where from the way he looks? And is he Muslim, and if so, what he is doing here on Christmas Day? It's Shimal who breaks the silence.

You come here often? he says, smiling at her.

Rosalind is caught off guard by the question. How is it that he – a what? an overseas student? a refugee? – is the one who seems to have the poise to lead conversation and the ability to wisecrack, while she – assured, capable, middle-aged, recently-retired professional woman – is at a loss and tongue-tied? She finds herself close to tears. She shakes her head. Shimal's expression changes immediately to one of concern.

Oh, I am very sorry. I don't wish to be rude. Only to make you feel easy. I know it is hard for a lot of people who come here today.

Rosalind fights for control. She nods. Shimal stands in front of her awkwardly. He reaches out an arm as if he would like to put it about her, but then lets it fall back to his side.

I will fill up our trolley, he says then. When I come back we finish the whole table, okay?

Rosalind nods and sniffles.

Shimal pulls out a chair for her, and she slides with relief into its hard embrace. The white tablecloth catches on her legs and pulls awry. Shimal straightens it and fusses around Rosalind.

I'm okay, she tells him. I'm okay.

Shimal wheels the trolley away. Rosalind lifts the side of the tablecloth and dabs at her eyes. She takes a few deep breaths. She isn't going to be able to do this, she thinks. She must get up and go out the door, back to the park, anywhere.

She can see, blearily, that a few other people have sat down here and there at the long tables. One man, dressed in a suit, has sat on the opposite side to her, a dozen or so chairs along. He appears to be talking to someone. Is he talking to her?

I'm sorry? Rosalind says but the man pays no attention.

He goes on talking, and now gesticulating. Perhaps he's wearing one of those mobile phone hands-free sets. But now he turns in Rosalind's direction and says very loudly, How can we know our true path? That's what I want to know. Will I recognise it when I see it?

Rosalind sniffles and thinks. She tries to formulate some kind of answer, but the man has turned away again and is continuing to speak to the air.

Shimal comes back with the trolley and puts a cup of tea down in front of Rosalind. This might help, he says. She smiles up at him. He pulls out the chair beside her and sits down.

This is your first time here? he asks gently.

Yes, she says. I usually have Christmas with my son. And you, you don't have anyone either? You usually help out for Christmas lunch?

Rosalind can't help noticing how black Shimal's skin is up close. And it has a sheen altogether different from skin like hers, like so-called white skin, which is more a pinkish, greyish brown. He smells of something sweet, some kind of scent, or incense.

I have been a volunteer for two years now, he said. Since I arrived.

Arrived from . . . ?

From Sudan. You know Sudan?

I know a little.

We have a very long civil war there. I joined the rebels when I was thirteen. It was very bad. It is still bad there. Especially in some parts. I come here as a refugee.

And your family?

Shimal puts his head down and places his fingertips on the table as if he's about to play piano. He takes a few moments before answering.

My family all died. I think. Only my brother, I am not sure.

You're not sure?

No one knows. Many people are missing. It's very difficult. I keep hope in my heart for my brother.

Rosalind puts her hand over one of his where it is tensed on the table.

It's good that you keep hope, she says. You must keep hope.

She thinks of something else.

It's good that you come to help here. It's a good thing to do. I wish I had thought to do it before.

Shimal lifts his head. He looks around the room, which is filling now with people drifting in.

Before I come to Australia, Australia is the land of milk and honey. Not like my country full of trouble. Now I see Australia has its own troubles. But my own life is better here. I want to say thank you by helping.

Rosalind says again, It's a good thing to do.

She begins to stand.

No, says Shimal, you stay. I will finish.

Rosalind nods. She is happy to be told what to do. She *craves* being told what to do. She sees reindeer-woman on the other side of the room placing large boxes under the Christmas tree. The antlers get tangled up with the lower branches as reindeer-woman tries to stand again. For a moment there is a tussle as she tries to pull clear. The branches of the tree shake and the little lights momentarily stop their frenzied blinking altogether. Next moment reindeer-woman is free. Rosalind finds herself giggling. What is wrong with me? she thinks. A well-dressed, grey-haired man appears beside her. He pulls out the next chair and sits down. He smiles at her.

You are enjoying yourself already, he says with some kind of faint European accent. Czech? Hungarian?

Rosalind, she says holding out her hand.

Tay-oh, he says as he shakes her hand.

Rosalind looks puzzled. Tay . . . ?

God, he says then.

Oh, says Rosalind.

In English you say it Theo, he says.

Now he is grinning more than smiling.

Rosalind smiles at him. She is relieved. And suddenly feels almost light-hearted. The day is clearly going to be full of unexpected things.

What were you laughing about? Theo asks.

I was . . . She is about to point out reindeer-woman. Instead she finds herself saying, I was thinking about reindeer.

Ah yes, he says. Very beautiful creatures.

I once lived with reindeer herders, Rosalind says.

Theo looks at her carefully. You did? he asks. I think you do not have reindeer in Australia, he says. Then he laughs, Ah, but I did see reindeer in a paddock in the north recently. I was coming home on the coach and there was a Santa and sleigh up on a rooftop. And next moment there was a paddock of reindeer. Real reindeer!

Rosalind stares at him. She is not sure if he is making up a story for her entertainment.

I think they farm them. For their velvet, Theo adds.

Rosalind's face lights up. You know about the velvet? she asks. Before Theo has a chance to answer she says, Not here. I mean when I was young. When I was young, I lived with the Saami people for a season. I was studying anthropology and I had this extraordinary opportunity. It was the experience of a lifetime. The children taught me how to lasso a reindeer. Imagine that! The children are taken out of school for the gathering of the herd. They call it reindeer school. I wasn't very good at it.

At anthropology? Theo asks.

Rosalind laughs. No, at reindeer lassoing!

Theo laughs along with her.

What an interesting life, he says. I would love to hear more.

It was thirty years ago now, she says dreamily. Her face lights up. Now I remember, she says. The Saami tell a story about an old man with a beard, who climbs into their tents through the cooking-smoke hole while they are sleeping. And brings the children presents!

Santa Claus, Theo says, has many guises.

Years later, they will laugh when they remember how surprised they were to look up and find all the long tables full. The level of noise from chatter could almost have been called a din. Theo had been telling her that he was a ceramicist back in Czechoslovakia when he was young. In Australia he'd worked in a factory making ceramic insulators. On the weekends they let him use the kiln for his own work. Now that he was retired, he'd built himself a kiln. I like to keep my hands in, he'd said spreading his palms as if for her inspection, in a gesture of pleading or offering. His wife died some years before and now his son lived in America, and his daughter was back in Czechoslovakia for Christmas.

And my son, Rosalind had begun.

Yes, Theo had said. Something made him reach out and take her hand in his.

My son died, she'd said at last. In a car crash. Last Christmas.

Theo had nodded and stroked her hand.

Bowls of soup are placed before them. Rosalind is taken aback.

I need to help! she says. I'm here to help! She half rises from her chair.

Theo places his hand on her arm. Keep me company, he says. Please.

Rosalind sits down. Shimal comes by with long baskets holding diagonally-sliced baguettes. He places a basket between Rosalind and Theo. He smiles at Rosalind.

Merry Christmas, Mrs Rosalind, he says.

Rosalind didn't know any smile could be so big. Merry Christmas, Shimal, she says.

When Shimal has moved on, Theo says, I've brought a book. I was thinking of going to the park to read after the lunch. Would you like to accompany me, I wonder?

Rosalind finds herself nodding so enthusiastically that she wonders if she, too, has reindeer antlers weighting her head. She reaches a hand up to check. To other people in the large, noisy hall it probably looks as if she is simply patting her hair.

Class of '73

She looks at herself in the mirror. The dress itself is beautiful. But it's got nothing to do with her. It sits there on her skin the way a rubber glove might. She's seen other women in dresses like this and they look as if they've been born in them, the way the fabric moulds itself against flesh and clings to hip bones. As if dress and woman are one. This looks like a borrowed dress. Which in a manner of speaking it is. Borrowed from that world of glossy magazines and elegant parties, from shops which make you feel like you need a new hairstyle just to go inside, let alone try anything on.

She'd felt quite brave the day she chose it. It made her feel powerful not to worry about the cost. She had more than enough money. All the same she was pleased the dress was half price. A designer label dress, no less. She doubts she's ever had one before. Although, when it comes right down to it, she doesn't understand that phrase. They all have labels don't they. They've all been designed. Somehow she thinks of it as being a dress which has been along a catwalk.

The thought makes her laugh and she turns from the mirror and sashays the length of the room. Sashays is the word, she thinks. Or something like that. Something which has the whisper of silk in it, the purr of the cat. She lets the unaccustomed high heels cantilever out her hips, imagines the complex interweaving arcs made through the air by her hip bones. She stops at the far wall, and puts her hands on her hips, does a full turn and pouts towards the seats where the fashion audience sits admiringly. Then she turns and works even harder on the hip sway as she walks back to the mirror.

Do models feel confident about the way they look from the back? She never has. Her one close friend from years ago always took up a brush as soon as they met and brushed the back of her hair. The friend always chided her for not taking enough care, not realising that those few brush strokes were something desired, consciously sought, the rare touch.

She takes the invitation from where it's tucked in the corner of the mirror frame. *Can you believe it? Thirty years since we graduated from high school!* She can believe it. There is something misty about those school years. Like going to the museum, which she usually does on Sundays, and looking through display glass with a layer of dust over it. It's all there, she knows it's there, but it's cloudy and she can't quite see it. On the other hand, if she closes her eyes, she can smell the canned tomato soup she used to have for lunch from the school canteen, can feel the absurd ungainliness of wearing thick socks over school shoes to save the floors. She can hear the exact pitch of the siren which called them inside. She can feel the flick of a boy's ruler under her skirt, the swift brush of breeze against her thighs. She can remember the faint arousal it brought on, that sudden heat inside her pants. She can feel it now.

An image jumps into her mind of a day on the beach. She went there with Sean McBride. They were an item for a little while after they finished school. They lay side by side on towels on the sand. He slid his hand underneath her and inside her bikini. She lay as still as still. It was as if the sun on her skin were making it happen, which made it all right. It was all she could do not to writhe. She almost managed to control her breathing but soon it changed pace and the woman closest to them on the sand picked up her infant child and hurried away with a deliberate sandy flick of her beach towel. Right there on the sand, Sean McBride gave her an orgasm. Her first. With a boy, anyway. She bit down against crying out and got her breathing back to normal. By her side Sean let out a small moan of his own. The whole time, she was facing the other way.

Oh my god, she suddenly thinks. What if he's there?

She'd forgotten all about that scrambly kind of going steady, furtive hands inside things, and nothing much said. Sex became so different later on. So easy. Too easy. Oh well, he probably wouldn't remember that particular episode even if he was there. And besides, it would be kind of interesting to see what he was like now. What any of them would be like.

Join us for a cocktail party at 5pm and take it from there! That was the word which made her rush out and buy the dress. Cocktail. What a word. Cock-tail! She has never actually been to a cocktail party and knew that nothing she had in her wardrobe would fit the bill. So she walked into the store and said she wanted a cocktail dress. This filmy, swingy dress with its shoestring satin straps is what she chose.

Will she tell them? she wonders. Will she tell them about her job? She could say that in some cultures her position would be esteemed, like that of a shaman or priestess, assisting the dead in their crossing from one world to another. In India, she is sure, she would be honoured for her work. Although – she frowns at herself in the mirror – did they need someone like her for cremations? Probably the preparation was done by family, the way it used to be here. She feels it as a privilege.

Being privy to the great mystery of life, something like that.

Anyway, who knows what the others will have done with themselves. There isn't a single one she's stayed in touch with. But then again, there aren't many live ones at all who she is in touch with. In touch. She sometimes wonders if it's the quiet of her work, the way she communes in silence rather than through endless chatter. Yes, she enjoys that.

The talk is what she fears. Small talk. And big talk. Ideas and books and travel. It isn't as if she hasn't travelled. She has. She's been to India. She's even swum in the Ganges for heaven's sake. She was booked into an ashram further north, but somehow never got there. The thought of all those other people with whom she was meant to strike up a relationship somehow put her off. So she stayed on in the city, drinking tea on the rooftop of her room, listening to the endless din made by so many people. She found she liked the anonymity. She told herself at the time it was meditative. She was going inside herself. That's what you did in India after all, didn't you? Some things filtered through to her despite her seclusion. Things about the class system that was supposed not to exist any more. She gleaned such things through overheard conversations, from the woman who came to clean and bring her meals. So what? There were unspoken class distinctions in this society. To do with social standing and education and employment. The day she bought the dress she overheard a well-dressed mother saying to her well-dressed daughter, who was trying to choose a jacket, that she thought the blue one was more classy. Classy. It has class. Funny way to put it.

She laughs as it occurs to her this is a *class* reunion. Class of '73. And she realises that, even at the time, at the age of fifteen, she could have accurately listed all her classmates in a social class hierarchy. The only one she would have had trouble placing was herself. Somewhere below the middle probably but not at the bottom. The one who was at the bottom, well, she doubts she'll be there tonight. And now she herself could be labelled untouchable. Someone who does the dirty work.

Untouchable. The word wounds. The last to touch her was her niece, her sister's daughter. Whenever she visited she would take the skin of her aunt's elbows between thumb and finger and laugh out loud at the way the skin pinched out and only slowly returned to its original shape. In the end this became just too tiresome to stand. They lost touch.

She pinches the skin of her left elbow now. Yes, despite her lotions and oils, the skin is like a piece of child's play dough left out overnight. It makes her think of the Hansel and Gretel story she used to read to that niece. As if she can be tested at the elbow to see if she's too tough to pop in the oven. But she is used to moulding skin which has lost its pliancy, gently patting and pushing a face into an expression of serenity or, at the very least, one relieved of the hard lines of pain. As for warm flesh, she wouldn't really know what to do with that in her hand any more. She has found herself wondering if, after all these years without being touched by a man, or anyone, let alone having sex, she might have returned to a state of virginity. Now that would be a good question for the nuns.

Surely they won't have asked the nuns along. They'd be too old. Or dead. A feeling of panic strikes her. Look at this dress, revealing her neck, chest, shoulders, arms. Its wafty fabric clinging to her shape. Her shape a little too curvaceous. She wouldn't call it fat. But fleshy, yes. No nun could approve of that. Flesh was a word they weren't keen on. But no, not one of those girls would have invited a nun. She's certain of it. All the same, the dress might not be the thing. After all it is a cocktail party in this town. It isn't Sydney or London. People will probably drink beers and wear jeans.

She worries now, thinking how terrible to be the only one dressed to the nines. Dressed to kill. That would be very uncomfortable. She doesn't want to stand out. That's why she bought the dress in the first place, to blend in by having an outfit appropriate to the occasion. She was hasty. It was the word which bamboozled her. Cock. Tail. Tall clinky glasses full of drinks in exotic colours, decorated with pieces of fruit and fancy swizzle sticks.

She catches sight of the clock on the wall. My god. Quarter to five. She needs to make up her mind. She pulls off the dress and rummages in a drawer for a shirt with three-quarter sleeves. Those elbows won't embarrass her. She grabs a pair of jeans, not her old blue jeans, but a dressy black pair. Dressy, yes, but she couldn't call them classy. Not in a million years. She looks at herself critically in the mirror. Now she looks plain fat instead of fleshy, rolls of black cotton gathering at her thighs.

The uncomfortable feeling in her stomach takes her right back to high school. The night of a school dance. The dread about what to wear. Her mother telling her it's not what you wear on the outside but what you're like on the inside that counts. The trouble was she felt even less confident about the inside although she couldn't tell her mother that. She wishes her mother were here now to say something soothing. She conjures up an image of her, the last image, at the chapel viewing. Whoever got her ready did a lovely job. There suddenly seemed so much to tell her. These days she talks to her people, and wonders if their loved ones have said the things they wished. In her experience, there was hardly ever time.

Her partner for the first dance that night was chosen by drawing names from a hat. She drew the shortest boy in the class. The shortest straw. His name was Darren. She's distracted by wondering how many people will take partners tonight. Even if they have them, they might not bring them. It wouldn't be much fun. People would end up saying, *You had to be there*, all night. Explaining. She sent back the form with the box ticked for one person.

A few years later, soon after she began her work, Darren came to her. He'd been in a motorcycle accident. She was shocked to see him. If he were able to go tonight, he'd probably be the tallest of them all. Gone from boy to man in a few years. And his body, as she dressed it, so very beautiful. She apologised to him for being ashamed of him the night of the dance. She wishes she could dance with him tonight and make up for it. She wonders all of a sudden if anyone else will be missing like Darren. Really missing. Missing in action.

A quarter to six. Well, she doesn't want to be the first one there. What if no one recognised her when they came in? Better to slip in among everyone quietly. Perhaps a skirt that doesn't show those thighs.

The ring of the phone makes her jump. She looks at herself in the mirror and lets the machine answer. Music and a hubbub of talk in the background. Someone shrieks with laughter. *Pen!* a voice says. *Where are you,*

Pen? Did you remember it was at five? Maybe you've lost the invite or something and got mixed up. Anyway we're all here. You wouldn't believe it. It's so weird. Wait till you see everyone!

Turnip thighs, they used to call her, this woman on the phone and her friend. Then they'd pretend to be nice and say it was just puppy fat and she'd grow out of it. Her voice is exactly the same as thirty years ago.

She walks over to the fridge and takes out an open bottle of wine. Pours herself a drink. Better catch up, she thinks, or I'll be even more out of things. She'd always felt out of things, like she didn't quite fit. Her mother told her it was because she was special, chosen for something else, not just to be one of the crowd. When all she wanted was to be one of the crowd. Thank goodness you get over that stage, she thinks to herself. I'm pretty happy with myself these days. Independent, a job which keeps me in touch with people, even if they are deceased, money, my own house.

She takes a skirt from the closet. It's one she usually wears to work because it's loose and comfortable. She sniffs the fabric. She hardly notices the smell of the disinfectants any more, except first thing on a Monday morning. But she's seen people step away from her in the line at the supermarket. The skirt seems fine. She pulls off the jeans, puts on the skirt. Better. She pours another glass of wine, one eye on the clock. Twenty-five past six. That's okay. It will only take fifteen minutes to drive there.

The phone shrills again. The answering machine whirs and beeps. *Pen! It's the new place down by the water, round the front in the cocktail lounge. Did I say that before? Everyone's dressed up for the occasion. Can't wait to see if you still look the same.*

The background noise has increased in pitch and volume. How can they have so much to talk about? They never used to talk to each other so much at school, just stayed in their little impenetrable groups. *A penny for your thoughts, Penny*, they'd sing out as they walked past where she sat eating lunch by herself. *Not worth it!* someone else would say. She didn't know what it was it took to be part of these groups but, whatever it was, she never had it. She left that school and never looked back. One on one and naked was the way she fitted best. She soon learned that. She belonged when someone was inside her. There were a lot of lovers. And then – she can't pinpoint exactly when – it all stopped. They didn't notice her any more, they didn't take her home. Perhaps that was the disinfectants too. She gradually came to accept being alone. It was good. It was an absence of feeling left out. It was impenetrable.

Under the invitation is a streaky photocopy of a

photograph of the class of '73. She picks it up and looks, not for the woman on the phone, but for Darren. He's easy to spot, still in that final year the shortest by far. Now he would be head and shoulders above any of them. She kisses her finger and places it gently on his face. She knows for certain he wouldn't have gone tonight.

She takes off the skirt and blouse, lifts the cocktail dress up and smells it. She pulls it on over her head. *May I have the first dance, Darren?* she says into the mirror, and twirls away across the room, glass in hand, stopping only to bend down and unplug the phone.

Poem of the sea

In my makeshift bed on the floor in front of the fire, I lie awake and listen to the night sounds. House timbers creak and the roof realigns itself. Bettongs bound through dry grass. Possums thump down the musical scales of five galvanised water tanks. A slight wind rustles gum leaves and waves lap the shore. I am waiting to hear another sound, one which seems to come from across the water.

I pull on my worn green dressing gown and go to sit on the verandah, the better to hear. There it is, just audible above the wash of waves, a faint, frail singing, a poignant skirmish of notes like a sad lullaby.

Across the bay, over on the peninsula, a light flashes in a regular pattern. I count. One, two, three flashes. I count four and five in darkness, then the sequence begins again on six. I try to count precisely and keep time with the flashes. These lights are timed meticulously so that sailors, their land-hungry eyes full of salt rime and fear, can be certain of their whereabouts. The channel is narrow; the sailors must get their bearings before they try to enter the canal. To continue around the Tasman and Forestier peninsulas would mean extra hours along treacherous coast, sailing over the graves of many a sailor, sailing past the graves of many a convict. None chooses it willingly, though the men who fish those waters have no choice. But they go with knowledge sitting in the grooves on their brows; you see it if you watch them in Constitution Dock, coiling ropes, cutting bait, checking gear, as they ready themselves and their boat for the next run. Nothing is left to chance; one slip and theirs can become just another sad story told about the hook of land, and the waters around it, that yearns south to icebergs and penguins and regular showings of the aurora australis.

Does the singing come from the land on the other side of the bay, from the curved coast inside the hook? I know sound travels far and distinctly over water but surely not this far. It is a mystery, one which I have begun to savour in my solitude in this little wooden house. The sound does not disturb or frighten me; the opposite is true. Its plaintive, broken melody soothes.

When I first came to this bright, quiet, water place in need of solitude and time, the night sounds terrified me. Possums held a welcoming party on the water tanks and roof, and this wild drumming and unearthly squealing brought panic; I imagined a wild anger. Those first nights I had little sleep but now the sounds have become strands in the backcloth of night and do not drag me from my dreams. Sometimes it would be better if they did. Many of my dreams are perilous night journeys over sunken terrors and hidden fears. I wake in the early morning light and draw a deep draught of air, like someone who has almost drowned, thankful to have survived, shaken to some deep centre of being, but with the calm, full knowledge of being back, safe, alive.

Could it be a mermaid? Surely this must be the kind of song that tantalises and haunts, entices sailors. Standing out on the verandah in the night, I feel myself tempted to climb down the steep steps and wade into shallow water, pushing through stands of seaweed, heading towards the lilting sound. I imagine the luxury of giving in to the pull and lull of it, the luxury of letting water lap around limbs, flow into mouth and ears.

My practical self counters with other possibilities. Could it be some trick of wind over land, or the call of a strange water bird? These explanations do not seem equal to the eerie quality of the notes. Perhaps watery vibrations of whale song entering night air? Whales are beginning to return to the river at last, reclaiming old feeding grounds for their journey south, but if they were to venture into these shallow bays among unpredictable nooks and juttings, they would never find a way out to the open ocean.

Sliprails angle down into the sea from shaky, silver-timbered boatsheds, which clutter the shore of the bay. Mostly the rails are rusty orange-brown and eroded. The disused tracks gather drifts of seaweed, shells, feathers, and slivers of white wood against their warped sides. I often gather these sea-thrown things to arrange again on my window sill.

On some nights I imagine that a ghost train slips out from a tumbledown shed and eases silently over the tracks into clear water. Seaweed waves against its windows. Stingrays flap towards the glass then glide away. Schools of fish turn as one from the silent train. It crosses the sea bed to the hook of land, there to emerge and disappear into similar hideaways on that shore. I imagine it is the ghost whistle of this train I hear on the night air.

I think this song is teaching me that I must live with mystery.

Lately I have noticed a pile of stones next to one of the jetties that wobble out from shore. The stones could not have washed up in that formation; it is too symmetrical, too formal a shape, like a tall pyramid. Once my eyes have distinguished it from surrounding stones, it is impossible to miss. It is growing. Someone is building a tower of stones. I look each day. It gives me something to look forward to.

For days now, the foundations have rattled beneath my heels as air is flung northwards, garnished with pellets of ice which hit the windows and slide downwards, a slow, melting death on my little house beside the sea. Deep, dark clouds mass and move menacingly towards the room where I sit watching ocean and sky, buffeted by wind and too many emotions, solaced by red coals in the hearth and red wine in my glass. I am on an island of my own making here in the storm's path.

It is grey. It has been grey for days. The sea is crawling; the wind is tossing danger into the air. My skin is stretched by the tension in the air; I am a drum, waiting. I long for things to settle. I watch the tower. It has stopped growing, has lost its clear edges, but has not quite disappeared back into the chaos around it. It remains a small, deliberate ordering of things.

At last the bay becomes flat and opalescent. It is so still that reflections sit on the surface of the water. The wind has dropped away and it smells like summer. Detail has crept back into the landscape. I can see trees behind the beach at Lime Bay and green pasture running into yellow tussocks on the point at the far end of the bay. Gulls skim the glassy surface, beady eyes down amongst seaweed. A white-bellied sea eagle flaps to a haughty stop on a broken gum limb along to my right. Out beyond the cairn of stones, a cormorant dives into water so clear I can trace its path below the surface until it emerges and flies off towards the west. I watch two stingrays glide into the shallows and drift over the sandy bottom. This is what I have come for – peace, calm. I want to bathe in it.

Through the branches of gums I catch a flash of colour on the shore and then a boy appears walking unsteadily, barefoot, over the rocks. He goes straight to the pyramid of stones and stands looking at it, his head to one side. After the storm it is more mound than pyramid. He goes to the other side and inspects it closely. He begins clearing away rocks from the base. Then he picks up stones, one by one, turns them over in his hands, lets them fall, or places them carefully in position on the tower. Some of the discarded stones are tossed along the shore where they clatter onto others or ring against the old sliprails. Sometimes he throws them into the water and gulls flap away from the splash. The tower is now as high as his chest. From my eyrie on the verandah it looks precarious, as if the next high tide or wave curl will drag it down again.

Summer has arrived. The scent of eucalyptus is stronger and sheep on the hillside behind the house huddle together in tree shade. I see the boy climb onto the rickety jetty in front of the house where I think he is staying. He steps gingerly from one plank to another, testing each one before giving it his full weight. He looks too young to be here on his own – sixteen, perhaps seventeen. He is wearing baggy shorts and his legs are spindly white sticks from this distance. He pulls his T-shirt over his head then pulls off his shorts and stands at the end of the jetty in bathers. He can't possibly be thinking of swimming so early in the season. The boy stands poised for a moment, then throws himself into the water. The loud smack and splash send the gulls wheeling away to the beach further round the bay. He surfaces and gives a loud whoop and starts swimming madly in the direction the gulls have taken. His arms circle out of the water and over his head like some kind of paddle wheel that draws him through the water. He stops his headlong rush, turns towards open water and starts swimming south away from the shore. He is a strong swimmer.

When he is a long way out he stops and stays still in the water, turning to face the shore. I am aware that he must be able to see me from out there; I am a lone figure in bright colours against the silver greys of bush and house. So I stand and wave. He lifts one arm out of the water and waves in a big arc, backwards and forwards, backwards and forwards. I start to feel uncomfortable. He looks like someone who is drowning and waving for help. I panic. The boy starts to swim back towards the shore and I breathe relief and go back into the house.

The next day he is fishing from the jetty. I check the tower. He must have attended to it early for it is straight and tall. Stones have been added around the bottom, giving the structure a broader base. He will be able to make it much higher that way. I wonder if he'd let me help him, but I'm not sure how I would ask.

On the verandah the next morning, there is a big blue plate arranged with white fillets of flathead under a blue and white tea towel. On the plate is a note. It says, *I have bathed in the poem of the sea.*

The fillets smell of the sea. I haven't had fresh fish for a very long time. I have been living on supplies that I brought with me and occasionally driving along the dusty coast road to the general store near the canal for vegetables, milk and eggs. I fry the fish in olive oil with garlic for lunch and say a soft thank you to the boy.

I have bathed in the poem of the sea.

The line runs around my head all through the quiet day. It feels vaguely familiar. But perhaps it is just something the boy has made up. The poem of the sea. That's how it is for me. The sea is a metaphor for all things. It draws me into contemplation. It sneaks up on me and stuns me with beauty, appals me with ferocity. Some days I can read it again and again; some days I can't bear to look at it, but even then my gaze is beckoned. I am hypnotised by it.

That night the mermaid calls to me and this time I can make out some of the words. They are in French . . . *le poème de la mer*.

In the morning I go down to sit on the end of the jetty. The sea is limpid. The sun warms my skin. Gulls cry raucously as they glide overhead. I watch seaweed waving in the gentle undulations of the water. I wonder where the mermaid goes during the day. I almost don't admit it to myself, but I am hoping the boy will appear.

His tower is a little further along the shore to my right and before long I hear the clatter of rocks from that direction.

How were the fish? he calls after a while. He's clearly not in a hurry for company. Am I?

I turn and call out, They were delicious. That was very kind of you.

He shrugs his shoulders.

I caught a lot that day.

Anyway, thank you. And, I wanted to ask about that line you wrote. Is it yours?

We are some distance from each other. I am sitting at the very end of the jetty beside the ladder which gleams down into seaweed. But the air is so still our voices carry perfectly.

I wish, he says. No, it's Rimbaud. You know, the French poet.

Rimbaud, I think, that's it. Surely not many boys of this age read Rimbaud.

I thought it sounded familiar, I say. I must have read it a long time ago. Yes, it is very . . . apt.

Rimbaud is good for out here, he says.

Yes, he would be.

Poetry, I think. Another ordering of the chaos.

Have you been for a swim yet? he asks as he sets another stone into place.

No, not yet. It still feels pretty cold to me.

I suppose so, he replies. It's worth it, though. It's always worth it.

Mmm. Yes.

We lapse into silence.

When the sound of rock on rock behind me stops, I turn to see the boy hopping over stones towards the beach.

Come up for a coffee some time, I call out to him, and he turns and waves. Is that a yes?

Now the tower is not the only thing I look forward to.

It is a couple of days before he climbs the narrow steps up onto my verandah and knocks on the glass. I am reading and I look up, startled. He is smiling through the window.

I've come for that coffee, he says.

We take our cups and the coffee pot onto the verandah.

Quite a view, he says.

Yes, I love it. It's perfect. I can see your tower from up here.

So you can. It's almost finished.

How can you tell?

Oh, I can tell, he says and laughs. When it's finished I'll go back to town. I've just been here collecting my thoughts.

In writing?

No, nothing like that, he laughs. I only read poetry. Not write it. Just putting my thoughts in order, getting my head around something. You know? The stones seem to help.

He might be eighteen, I think as I listen to him, no more. There is something about him, a wry twist to his lips, the straggle of long blond hair, the squint of blue eyes, that I would guess was Australian if I saw him in another land. Australian, or from some other sea-drawn place.

Yes, I think I know. I'm getting my head around something, too, I say. The expression sounds much too young in my mouth. It sounds absurd. We laugh.

How's yours going? he asks with a grin.

Well, I'm working on it. We laugh some more. Laughter. What a long time it's been. What a luxury. It flows through my body like the warmth of wine. I feel it reach my fingertips. I am alive, after all. What a surprise.

He tells me his, but I don't tell him mine. Mine is an ordinary tale, a tale of loss, but one worn smooth by many tellings, many people. It is nothing new. She lost her husband, people will say. Just that. His tale is not at all ordinary.

He is in senior secondary school, getting ready to go to university. His great love at school is French. French poetry.

One day after school he is walking along the docks on his way to skateboard in one of the big warehouses when a car crosses his path, out of control, and bumps over the wooden edges of Constitution Dock and plunges into the water. He pulls off his shoes and dives into the water. He is a strong swimmer but he has desperation in his mouth, the taste of fear on his tongue. The water is murky. The car is white. He can see it and, inside it, movement. Then the movement becomes a thrashing as the window of the driver's door is pulled down and water surges in. He grabs the door and pulls it. The pressure against it is enormous. He gets it open. There is water and air and a woman in panic, her hair streaming around her. Her mouth is open to scream something to him. She struggles. She fights him as he tries to pull her away towards the surface. She is holding onto the car and he realises there is someone else. He must get the woman up. She needs air. He needs air. He pulls her free and they rise to the surface. The woman goes limp. People are leaning over the side of the quay and another man jumps into the water to help the woman.

The boy takes a breath. His heart is banging. He dives down again and now the car is full of water. He can't see into the back seat. He pulls on the back door but it is locked. He pulls himself into the front seat. There is a baby in the back in a baby seat, a baby with its eyes closed as if it were napping. He tries to undo the seat buckle but can't see how it works. He pulls at the straps. He tries the buckle again. Someone else is there in the water now. A girl. She gets the other back door open. The girl is inside the car and has got the baby out of the seat. She passes the baby to him and he pushes out and up to the surface. Now there are people in a boat. He hands the baby up to them. An ambulance screams up to the dockside and paramedics take over. The mother and child are loaded into the ambulance and driven away.

She died, he tells me speaking quietly. Drowned. I keep imagining those baby lungs filling with water. Such tiny lungs, it wouldn't take long. I can't get them out of my mind. I didn't save her. I went to the hospital and saw the mother. She thanked me, but I could see in her eyes that she felt ambivalent about having survived.

I couldn't talk to anybody about it, he continues. I couldn't study. I dropped out of school. I just kept replaying the whole scene over and over trying to see what I could have done better. I dreamt about it. Nightmares. You know.

I think, You did your best. You tried. You saved the mother's life. What if you hadn't been there at all? But I bite down on my platitudes and can find nothing else to offer.

So. That's what I've been trying to get my head around, he continues. I came out to the shack to think things through. Let them settle. Or anyway just to *be* for a while. My whole world had been turned over by what happened and I just couldn't accept it. I've had to try to forgive myself. To *learn* to forgive myself. That's what it's amounted to.

There's a long pause.

I did my best to save the baby. I know I did. And now I have to forgive myself somehow for not succeeding.

I nod.

The girl, he says then. The girl who dived in too. She rings me. We're going to meet up when I go back to town. Soon. Maybe.

The sun drops away behind the mountain and turns the underside of clouds to pink and gold. The tide has crept in and water sucks at the pylons and boards of the jetties, flows around the base of the cairn of stones. In the evening air the sea is flat and milky and our thoughts drift out over it, across the bay where the navigation light has started flashing. At any moment, I expect a frail tune to drift our way, but I hear only the sound of the sea.

Here be dragons

The tractor engine's burring has woven itself into her head, as if the plough is gently tracking over contours of her brain, turning soft, grey soil. Only a change of pitch at a shift in speed or direction brings it fully into consciousness as she goes about her chores. She imagines Robert sitting up on the Massey Ferguson concentrating on keeping the purr even and the furrows smooth and straight. Backwards and forwards, backwards and forwards. Like knitting, she thinks, or worry beads, or swimming laps of the pool the way she used to when they lived in the city.

She clears the table – mugs of half-drunk coffee and the baby's gnawed toast crusts. He is playing happily now on kitchen floorboards with cake tins, wooden spoons and a plastic spatula. She puts on a load of washing, then throws chicken carcasses in a pot on the stove for stock. One basket of washing sits waiting to be pegged out. She has studied today's weather charts. The wind will arrive soon, swirling around the high pressure system. Good for drying, but dust from the ploughed paddock will be blowing straight this way.

There's talk in the area of cloud seeding. What does it mean exactly? She has an image of school children scattering seeds on wet cotton wool and waiting for them to grow into a pale thatch of stems. She remembers the town children's laughter the day she told them she'd brought rape seed. Now they call it canola.

She looks out the window to where the red tractor never stops. Dark, turned earth reflects little sunlight so the ploughed part of the paddock is bathed in a calm clear light. In the big unploughed section dry brittle grass dazzles. She has to shade her eyes. She read the other day that it's called albedo – how much light bounces off a surface. She thinks of a boyfriend she had once at uni – a dark-skinned Samoan – and how they used to joke on the beach that he should move out of the way because he was absorbing all the light.

In the night she had dreamed that her father came to visit them on the farm. They knew it was for one day only and they had a lot to catch up on. Four years. He was surprised by many things. To find them here at all. Farming. Robert farming. He was a city boy, a counsellor, university trained. He'd never so much as pulled a thistle. And the baby. A grandson. Well, that took the cake.

She showed him around, showed him changes they'd made. But some things remained the same. His ancient cows were still breeding. She told him about next door's stud bull breaking through the fence and pointed to the new calves. Obviously he'd been more attractive than their own old bull. Her father had chuckled off and on for hours over that. Said perhaps they shouldn't repair the fence too well.

He was pleased to see all the sheds his own father built still standing. She didn't tell him that one was now empty. It used to contain a half-assembled wagon, its iron wheels at the ready. Her grandfather had built wagons. But after long deliberation she and Robert had decided to sell it to a museum which was offering a big price. The money would help to buy feed for the animals. Dry weather was taking its toll. They didn't call it drought. Not yet.

Her father lifted a handful of soil and let if drift though his fingers, tut-tutting. She didn't tell him she had become obsessed by the weather, studying the charts, never missing a forecast on the radio or the television. And trawling the internet for information. Which has led to other obsessions. Her father was amazed to see a computer on his old desk.

When she woke, the realisation gradually dawned that she'd been dreaming. Then she spotted her father's jumper lying on the floor by the bed and for one moment wondered if it was real after all. But she had thrown it there herself last night. She'd taken to wearing his old jumpers outside. She'd never thrown them out and his smell was still in them four years on. She will probably never wash them.

Today she finds that she slips into thinking it is her father out there on the tractor. And as she mixes a batch of scones she suddenly becomes her own mother and the baby on the floor is her. She grips the mixing bowl. That tractor is messing up her brain. She roughly scrapes the dough from her fingers and scrubs her hands under the cold tap until they ache. Turning up the red palms she looks at her hands. It's hard to believe these hands once worked for hours over difficult pieces of music, starting with the hardest section and taking two bars at a time, building up the left hand, slowing everything right down until she didn't falter, always pushing herself. She remembers the monotony. But she also remembers achievement and the vibration of a dwindling note under the tip of a finger. In the light from the kitchen window she examines her fingertips, the whorls and hachures of each print. We are all different, she tells herself. I can never become my mother. I am me.

She studies more closely the print of her right middle finger, mesmerised by its arches and loops. Years ago on

Sardinia an Italian man told her that they call this one the wedding finger. At the time, she didn't think that could be right. She explained to him the wedding finger was the one on which you wore your wedding band. But later that night, after they'd danced and drunk a bottle of local red wine and walked up into the stony fields, he showed her what he meant.

She laughs as she notices the unconscious gesture she has made with her middle finger. Reassured, she goes back to the bowl and pulls the dough together.

Later, tidying away toys in the loungeroom, she looks up at the photograph of the farm which has hung above the fireplace since she was a child. It is really a photograph of the farmhouse and a few surrounding paddocks. She remembers when her parents got it.

An enterprising crop duster had seen an opportunity to make money. He realised he was one of the few ever to view from above the works of art created by farmers on the canvas of their farms. He got really revved up about it and started taking a photographer up with him. What cockie, he asked himself, could pass up the chance to have an aerial view of his farm? Candy from babies, he told the photographer.

The pilot turned up unannounced one day with the black and white print and told her parents that it would be coloured with inks if they agreed to purchase it, which they immediately did. She trailed after him as he went about making intricate colour notes. He also told her parents that he could touch up anything they weren't happy with about the photograph, tamper a little with reality. They asked him to get rid of the stock truck parked by the sheds and erase the cattle crammed in the yards ready for the sales. They asked him to close the white gate their daughter had left open, yet again, on her morning walk to the school bus. She never expected to be caught out so blatantly.

Gazing at the photograph she realises how similar it is to her own mental map of the farm. The farmhouse is central, then sheds, barn, home paddocks. After that, detail peters out, colours are less differentiated, and finally the rest of the property is outside of the frame. Here be dragons, she says. It reminds her of old maritime charts she's seen on which coastlines, harbours and rivers are densely detailed but hinterlands blank. Only the relevant is mapped. Her farm, she realises, begins and ends within a small radius of the house. This is her domain.

Maps, of late, obsess her. The weather maps began it, with their isobars and fronts and troughs. She has become accustomed to their iconography and sees straight away what's in store. Her favourite word is hectopascal. But on the internet she has also discovered geographical maps. Perhaps rediscovered is truer for she was an avid map reader as a child. She is particularly intrigued by the many maps she finds of their locality – physical, climate, vegetation, land use. They are marked as food and forage.

She realises the map of this place she has carried from childhood has been emotional rather than scientific. She could take the icons of cartographers and create a personal legend. A mulberry tree here, a spider's web there. She thinks of abstract maps, ones important to her, which take their metaphors from nature – the family tree, the World Wide Web. If I could map my life, she asks herself, what would it look like? Would it be a contoured skin bearing icons of its past, a seismographic chart of movement and now stillness, a graph of successes and failures? Or would it come down to a fingerprint?

She watches her baby begin his own map making, trotting on all fours beyond the frame of the known. She has spent the entire day alone but for him. She did not expect this. Was it this way for her mother? Thank goodness for email and the internet. She emails her friends in the city regularly. They tell her about the latest developments at work, about promotions, about new restaurants, films and plays they've been to, and new lovers. What can she tell? About the cow giving birth to twins? The calf which got caught in a gully and died? That a possum comes every night to bounce down their roof? About the fig jam she's made to her mother's handed-down recipe? The mulberry stains which took so long to disappear from those whorls on her fingertips?

She could tell them she's learned a new software program to do the accounts, sought out websites on the current price of beef and potatoes, mixed the feed for the calves she rears by hand. She could tell them it's all different than she'd imagined. That having a child and being isolated has kept her in the house and yard and in the traditional roles she has always shunned. That days and days go by without her speaking to anyone other than Robert. That she's tied to her own apron strings.

She could say how Robert has taken to it, not like a duck to water exactly, but with persistence, even stubbornness. Characteristic of everything Robert does. She knows it is for love of her. It was she who wanted to come back to the farm. But she didn't expect to feel so excluded. He doesn't seem to need her. When the tractor won't go he consults the manual and works it out for himself. When an animal is sick he rings and talks to the vet with whom he's become friends. He keeps his own counsel nowadays.

They've been lucky. Just as they got established on the farm, beef prices soared as Britain's foot and mouth put it out of the market. They invested in more stock, Robert poring over books at night and talking to neighbours about what to look for. Soon he could judge a calf's weight and health at a glance, like an old hand. Local farmers gave grudging approval. For a city boy he wasn't doing badly.

Robert knows they are keeping a close eye, waiting for him to make a slip. It isn't malice or meanness. It is simply a way of reminding themselves that, although they don't have a certificate in a fancy frame, they know a lot. It is a different kind of knowing, one lodged in creases on the forehead, in scars and calluses. It is hard-earned and very quiet.

Suddenly she is aware that she can't hear the tractor. She looks out but it has become dark without her noticing. She turns on some lights and gathers the baby up from the floor. She goes to the porch and calls. A faint answer from the direction of the newly-ploughed home paddock.

When Robert appears at the door she is shaken. His eyes are wide and staring and he teeters as he stands there, grim-faced.

What is it? she asks.

He puts both hands against the door jambs to steady himself.

I thought I'd do a few more runs before the light went. I finished one pass and turned but darkness had dropped just like that. I turned too wide and lost the edge I'd ploughed to. I drove all over that paddock looking for it but I couldn't find the edge. I finally stopped, turned her off and walked towards the house lights.

Are you all right?

When I stopped it was as if she went on moving and the noise kept on in my ears. I could hardly walk straight. I feel . . .

She takes his hands down from where they are braced and stills him in her arms. She leads him into the bedroom.

I feel woozy.

She tends him the way she tends the baby, removing shoes, trousers, underclothes. Everything is layered with a thick grime of sweat and dust. The exposed parts of his body are the exact colour of the paddock he has ploughed. She wipes his face. She tucks him into bed and brings him water. He doesn't want food.

You overdid it, she says after a while.

It's as if I hypnotised myself, he says. Back and forth, back and forth.

You should vary it, she says. Go round and round, make waves, doodle. You take it too seriously.

He looks at her and she looks away.

The next morning Robert is still dazed and disoriented. He says it must have been the sun. He stays in bed. He is disappointed that he will not be able to plough the front paddock as planned. He knows that neighbours would have driven by, dropping their speed at one end of the paddock to see what a job he was making of it. This is what he's been preparing for, over months. The front paddock. He'd show them. But not today. He wonders vaguely if anyone will notice the meandering tyre tracks from the night before.

She checks the charts first thing. Rain. Tomorrow. At last. But it is always too much or too little or the wrong time for farmers. If the front paddock isn't ploughed today it could be weeks before they have another chance. She sits at the breakfast table, spooning soggy Weet-Bix into her son's mouth. By the time they reach the bottom of the bowl she has a plan.

Usually she uses the baby backpack for walks. Occasionally she has used it on the four-wheeler motorbike when she's gone off to open a gate for stock or to take Robert some lunch. The baby loves it and gurgles happily as she straps him in.

She finds the tractor not far from the ploughed edge amid a crosshatching of tracks. He really was lost. She climbs on and sits there letting the feel of it sink in. For a moment her father's arms are about her waist. Turn her, he's saying, turn her hard.

Cars slow at the driveway fence. Some go so far as to stop. It is not the sight of the woman – old Merv's daughter, you remember – or even the small head peeping from the pack on her back. It is the odd manner in which she is ploughing the front paddock. Not a straight line in sight. Waves and whorls, arches and loops. You reckon she's drunk? Mad? But she's handling the tractor well, you have to give her that.

One more loop, she says to the baby, and we're out of here.

The baby hasn't got a clue but laughs to hear the new bright tone in his mother's voice.

[illegible]

[illegible]

[illegible] like to [illegible]

[illegible] for their [illegible]

[illegible]

[illegible] Christie [illegible]

Acknowledgments

I would like to thank Louise Oxley and Adrienne Eberhard for their unflagging belief that these stories could become a book. And my thanks to Madonna Duffy and Christina Pagliaro at UQP for turning them into one.

[illegible] first [illegible]

[illegible] Harvest [illegible] prize in the [illegible]
[illegible] Short Story [illegible]

[illegible] was highly [illegible] commended [illegible] WA
[illegible] Haddon [illegible]
[illegible] House [illegible]

[illegible] Sugar [illegible]
[illegible] was published in [illegible]
[illegible] surprise [illegible] list in the [illegible]
[illegible] Short Story Competition [illegible] was
[illegible] published in *Island* [illegible]
[illegible] Nation [illegible]
[illegible] Princess' [illegible]
[illegible] story competition [illegible]
[illegible] third prize [illegible] Short Story
[illegible]

The stories

'Camera Obscura' was published in *Verandah*.

'Blood Harvest' won second prize in the My Brother Jack Short Story Award 2002 and was published in *Meanjin*.

'Sojourn' was highly recommended in the FAWWA Lyndall Haddow Short Story Award 2006.

'Kafka's House' won the Shoalhaven Literary Award 2005.

'How Much Sugar?' was published in *Overland*.

'Pram Rage' was published in *Scarp*.

'Surprise, surprise' was a semi-finalist in the HQ/Harper Collins Short Story Competition 1997 and was published in *Island*. It was also broadcast on ABC FM and Radio National.

'Emerald Princess' was winner of the R. Carson Gold Short Story competition 2005.

'Ice' won third prize in the My Brother Jack Short Story Award 2000 and was published in *Island*.

'Class of '73' was winner of the My Brother Jack Short Story Award 2004 and was published in *Best Australian Stories 2004* (Black Inc, 2004). It was also broadcast on ABC FM and Radio National.

'Here Be Dragons' won second prize in the My Brother Jack Short Story Award 2003 and was published in *Famous Reporter*.

Other stories in this collection are previously unpublished.

Other titles by Kathryn Lomer

THE GOD IN THE INK

Claire's childhood is shaped by the Tasmanian farm she knows and loves. As an ex-POW, her father has struggled to return to a normal life through working the farm, and Claire has always assumed she will run the property herself one day. When there appears to be little chance of that, she looks elsewhere for an understanding of self and home.

Japan seems an unlikely place to discover a sense of identity. Claire finds a way into the culture through the Zen art of ink painting, and her dreams take on a new shape when she meets Toshiyuki. His mother had left post-war Japan for Paris, and Toshi is searching for his own cultural roots.

Together Claire and Toshiyuki try to make sense of their personal and family histories and create their own ways of belonging. But the past has a habit of reappearing to define the present.

The God in the Ink is a warm, beguiling novel of great beauty. Kathryn Lomer combines a novelist's sense of pace with a poet's fine ear for language.

ISBN 978 0 7022 3210 7

UQP

THE SPARE ROOM

This family, she said very slowly, is the Titanic. *She looked up at me and added something about an iceberg.*

Journeys take on many forms . . .

Akira is sent by his family in Japan to learn English in Australia, a journey into a world very different from his own.

Akira's homestay hosts, the Moffat family, are not quite what he was expecting. But then, what does he know about Australians?

In this tender and evocative tale, Kathryn Lomer takes us into two cultures, into lives connected by grief and uncertainty but with hope in common. It is the story of a journey into belonging, understanding and empowerment.

. . . and the first steps are often the hardest.

ISBN 978 0 7022 3477 4

UQP

TWO KINDS OF SILENCE

I would like to sit with you in the depths
of black water, up to my neck in it,
the pebbles on our tongues, in our palms
and pockets, arms around you,
hands under you,
to lift you up
into the living air

Bold, musical, lively and highly alluring, *Two Kinds of Silence* invokes not only the splendour of the Tasmanian coastline and hight country, but also the fire and reach of imagination, the poignancy of parenthood, and the overwhelming force and consequence of adult love. Kathryn Lomer's poems prove her to be richly inspired.

ISBN 978 0 7022 3612 9

UQP